"Did you think you could escape me?"

Chloe was unable to answer Leon's question—and just as powerless to stop his assault upon her senses.

His thumb caressed the curve of her mouth, and her lips parted instinctively, her flesh tingling beneath his touch. "Leon, stop it!" she pleaded. His tongue probed her earlobe, and her feeling of lethargy increased. Heat and shame washed over her, her agonized protest silenced as the thumb that had been stroking her lips into pliable softness was removed and Leon's mouth came down on her own, obliterating reason and pride. Her lips parted beneath his in mindless surrender, her small moan lost under the crushing weight of his body as he joined her on the settee, the warmth of his body against hers turning her lassitude into aching desire....

Books by Penny Jordan

Harlequin Presents

These books may be available at your local bookseller.

For a free catalog listing all titles currently available, send your name and address to:

Harlequin Reader Service
2504 West Southern Avenue, Tempe, AZ 85282
Canadian address: Stratford, Ontario N5A 6W2

PENNY JORDAN

island of the dawn

Harlequin Books

TORONTO • NEW YORK • LONDON
AMSTERDAM • PARIS • SYDNEY • HAMBURG
STOCKHOLM • ATHENS • TOKYO • MILAN

Harlequin Presents first edition November 1983
ISBN 0-373-10641-6

Original hardcover edition published in 1982
by Mills & Boon Limited

CHAPTER ONE

SHE would have to go back to the hotel and face Derek sooner or later, Chloe acknowledged grimacing slightly. At this early hour she had the beach to herself, but soon it would start to fill up with other holidaymakers. They had chosen this particular island deliberately because it was so small. There they would find the time and tranquillity to develop their relationship, Derek had told her, but she hadn't realised then that the developments he had in mind entailed her sharing his bed. Oh, she wasn't naïve; their friendship couldn't have remained platonic for ever, but she had never given Derek the slightest indication that by coming on holiday with him she was willing for them to be lovers. It only went to show how little one really knew about people one saw every day, Chloe reflected. She and Derek had worked together for eighteen months, and she had been drawn to him by his air of solid dependability, his conversation's lack of sexual innuendo. Their friendship had developed slowly over the months they had known one another, and Chloe had felt no qualms or inner warnings at all when Derek had suggested they spend their summer holiday together. A mistake, as she now acknowledged. She *had* been a little concerned when he suggested Greece, but had stifled her fear by reminding herself that she couldn't go on refusing to visit such a beautiful part of the world simply because of something which was over and done with for good.

5

She lifted her head, unaware of the attractive picture she made in her brief white shorts and thin cotton top. Her skin was already faintly tanned, the warm colour emphasising the silver fairness of hair which reached well below her shoulders in a heavy cascade. She lifted one slender arm to push her hair out of her eyes, unconscious grace in the simple movement. Normally for the office she wore her hair up. Perhaps she was to blame for Derek's behaviour after all, she reflected with a touch of wry humour. Wasn't there something in the Bible about the dangerous enticement of unbound hair? Just another example of the male sex's ability to blame women for their own failings!

One or two people stopped to greet her as she walked leisurely back towards the hotel complex. Although she and Derek had only arrived the previous day, Chloe's graceful carriage and strikingly attractive features made her instantly recognisable—something she had become accustomed to during the days she had worked as a model for a Paris fashion house. Not that Monsieur René would employ her now, she thought ruefully. It was true that her legs and waist were still as slender as ever, but maturity had brought a seductive swell to the breasts and hips which at eighteen had been almost unnoticeable.

In the hotel foyer overhead fans reminiscent of a turn-of-the-century film setting cooled the air. The hotel was one of the most luxurious Chloe had ever stayed in. Derek had chosen it, and although for herself she would have preferred something a little simpler she had made no demur, agreeing with him that for privacy one had to pay, and Thos island certainly guaranteed that. The hotel was the only one on the small Aegean island, and since, by modern standards, it was not a huge, soulless mass of sprawling concrete, but a tastefully designed and carefully laid out complex containing everything the discerning holidaymaker could want for his comfort, it was obviously proving very popular. A lucrative venture for whoever had financed it, Chloe reflected absently as she asked for her key, and debated the advisability of telephoning Derek from her own room, or going straight to his to see if he was up. By nature she was inclined to say what she thought and act accordingly and was inclined to expect others to do the same—an error she had fallen into too often. She ought to have made it abundantly clear to Derek before they came away that holidaying together, while it might further their friendship and enable them to get to know one another better, was not an invitation to him to share her bed.

Last night had been an eye-opener in more ways than one. He had sulked like a small child when she told him that they weren't going to become lovers. Her soft mouth compressed in a firm, straight line as she remembered some of his remarks.

'It isn't as if you were a virgin!' he had thrown furiously at her—as though that fact in itself by some unwritten law conferred a right on every man she met to sleep with her as and when the fancy took him. The young Greek boy behind the reception desk watched her in covert admiration. Her hair was the colour of the fine pale grains of sand on the beach, and her eyes as deeply amethyst as the sea just before sunset. Chloe glanced up and saw the way his eyes lingered on her breasts before he looked away, and her mouth compressed a little more. Damn Derek!

Damn all men, especially....Like a well-trained animal her mind veered away seeking other channels. For her the old adage 'What can't be cured must be endured' held a wealth of meaning, and when she had found it impossible to endure she had simply built a wall and locked away behind it the uncurable and the unendurable.

She would ring Derek from reception, she decided, reaching for the courtesy telephone. She was in no mood to endure another lengthy tirade, to hear him last night anyone would have thought that she was reneging on a bargain. She should have listened to Hilary, her flatmate, she acknowledged grimly. Hilary had warned her that there was more to Derek's suggestion than met the eye, but Chloe had blithely ignored her. Because she hadn't wanted to believe her, she admitted now. She had wanted this holiday, wanted and needed it. Her job in the public relations firm where Derek was an accountant was an arduous one and she had been reluctant to go away alone. As she had learned from bitter experience, a woman alone was like game in the open season where some men were concerned—men who simply refused to believe that a woman would go away alone simply to be *alone*. The simple truth was that she had agreed to go with Derek because he represented protection, ignoring Hilary when she pointed out that she might find that Derek might have ideas of his own. They were just good friends, she had stressed, ignoring Hilary's unkind hoot of laughter. If Hilary hadn't been planning her wedding the two of them might have been able to go away together. At twenty-three Chloe was beginning to find that the majority of her girl-friends were no longer single, while she herself. . . .

Her fingers trembled as she dialled Derek's room number. Heavens, what was happening to her? She mustn't think of that now. She had put it all behind her and that was where it was going to stay. Where it had to stay for the sake of her sanity.

There was no reply from Derek's room. Puzzled, Chloe hung up. Perhaps he had already come down for breakfast? They had arrived at the hotel only the previous afternoon by boat from Piraeus and Derek had suggested that they have an early night. That had been when the quarrel started as Chloe remembered it.

'The *kyria* is worried? Something is wrong?' the young Greek asked her hesitantly.

He was good-looking as only young Greek boys can be, small and slim with liquid dark eyes and white teeth in a healthily tanned face.

'Mr Simpson doesn't seem to be in his room,' Chloe told him. 'I expect he's gone into breakfast without me. I'll go and look for him.'

To her surprise the boy frowned, shaking his head from side to side vehemently, which she already knew in Greece signified a negative response.

'The *kyrios* has left,' he informed an astounded Chloe. 'He went this morning. I have here his key.' As though challenging her to disbelieve him he produced a key from the cubbyholes behind him. It was Derek's, but Chloe felt sure the boy must have made a mistake. Derek had probably just gone out for a walk as she had done herself.

'He can't have left,' she insisted calmly. 'We only arrived yesterday. Perhaps you misunderstood.'

'No misunderstand,' the boy insisted stubbornly.

'He come down this morning early and ask for the documents he place in safe keeping. I give them to him and he asks what time the boat goes to Piraeus. I tell him, and he say to have his bags collected from his room.'

A cold, sinking feeling had taken possession of Chloe's stomach. Surely Derek would never go to such lengths simply because of their quarrel? He was not like that. Or was he? Did she really know him at all? A man who coolly expected a girl to sleep with him simply because they were on holiday together—and Chloe had paid for her own holiday—and then spent the entire evening sulking because she refused. But to forfeit his own holiday. . . .

Stop panicking, Chloe told herself. There was a simple explanation for all of this. There had to be. Derek simply could not leave—for one thing, her passport had been in that envelope in safe keeping, and her travellers' cheques. She started to shake as the consequences of Derek's actions began to reach her. The young Greek boy, alarmed by her pale face and bemused expression, retreated to an office off the reception and returned accompanied by a plump middle-aged man.

'*Kyria*, I am the manager. Stephanos tells me that you are concerned that your friend has left. . . .'

'You mean that he *has* left?' Chloe demanded, only half aware that she was being dexterously escorted through the busy foyer to a small private room, luxuriously furnished as an office with cool floor tiles and heavy masculine furniture. For some reason the office filled her with a sense of atavistic dread, but she pushed the sensation aside. She must get to the bottom of Derek's outrageous behaviour.

'I regret that this is so,' the manager told her, eyeing her curiously. 'Please sit down, *kyria*. Would you like something to drink? Our sun can have ill effects on those not used to it. Have you had breakfast?'

'Did he leave anything for me? A package? A note?' Chloe asked, without any real hope of an affirmative answer. She knew already by some extra sense that Derek, in the same mood of spiteful bitterness which had prompted him to leave, had taken with him her passport and travellers' cheques.

'If you will excuse me I shall check,' the manager said formally.

He was gone just long enough for Chloe to study her surroundings a little more closely. They were both elegant and expensive, and there was no reason for her to experience this fear that in some way they threatened her, and yet she did.

She knew the moment the manager opened the door that Derek had left her nothing, and the full enormity of her situation dawned. She had no money to speak of, and far more important, no passport. Oh why, oh why had she so blithely agreed to Derek's suggestion that they simply share the envelope to be placed in safe keeping? Why had she allowed him to persuade her into handing over her passport at all? Why hadn't she kept it? Because she had simply not thought. Derek had suggested that placing it in safe keeping was the sensible thing to do, and she had agreed.

She glanced down at her hands folded loosely together, right over left, the fingers of her right hand holding her ring finger. It was a defensive pose she remembered well from those first bleak months when the pain in her heart was as raw as the tender skin where her wedding ring had once been. Now the defensive movement was a symbolic one only, for there was no band of pale skin to betray the fact that she had once worn a man's ring on that finger. A band of gold linking together two hearts and two bodies, or so she had romantically thought on the day it was placed there. She should have learned her lesson then. No man was to be trusted. Not a single, solitary one. Well, she was well served by her own stupidity now—trapped on a tiny Greek island with something like ten pounds in her bag and no passport. What did one do in such circumstances? Vague thoughts of approaching the British Consul flitted through her mind, only to be instantly dismissed as she acknowledged that somewhere as tiny as Thos which didn't even run to a tourist information office was hardly likely to possess anything as grand as a British Consul. It wasn't even as though she were on the type of package holiday where one could appeal to the representative of the tour operators; Thos and the hotel were too small for that kind of thing. What on earth was she to do?

The first and most sensible course of action seemed to be to confide in the manager, which Chloe did, skirting lightly round the reason for Derek's sudden departure with her passport and travellers' cheques, but she suspected from the sudden gleam in his eyes that he knew there was more to the story than she was telling him.

'The *kyrios* was not affianced to you?' he asked smoothly when Chloe had finished. 'There was no. . . .'

'He was a friend—nothing more,' Chloe retorted

more sharply than she had intended. 'And a very poor friend, as it now turns out!'

'A bad friend is more dangerous than a thousand enemies,' the hotel manager remarked sapiently. 'Although it might be possible for you to leave Thos without your passport, the authorities in Athens would not let you leave the country. I shall speak to my head office in Athens, to see what is to be done, and meanwhile I suggest you fill in a form I will give you—for the authorities, you understand.'

The form was long and detailed and the manager explained that it was one normally used if tourists lost any item of luggage or other personal belongings. The amount of detail seemed incredible to Chloe, but knowing how sensitive Greeks could be to criticism she refrained from saying anything, hesitating only when it come to 'Married Status' before writing quickly with a grimace of distaste 'Separated' and then hurriedly folding the paper.

When he returned the manager suggested that she might care to go and have a belated breakfast, but Chloe had no appetite for food. Instead she returned to the beach, avoiding the convivial crowds already gathering round the huge, Olympic-sized swimming pool.

Only when she had reached the far end of the curving bay, almost out of sight of the hotel, did she stop, sitting with her knees drawn up under her chin as she stared out to sea, memories which had been pursuing her for two years suddenly breaking past the barriers she had erected against them to come flooding into her mind with their bitter legacy of pain and anguish. She should never have come back to Greece, she acknowledged. It acted as too powerful a stimulant on her mind. True, Thos was not Rhodes, and Derek not Leon, but when Derek had tried to kiss her last night, forcing the unpleasant moistness of his mouth on hers, it had triggered off the memories, especially of that last awful quarrel when Leon had practically tried to rape her and then accused her. . . . She shivered suddenly despite the heat of the sun.

She had been twenty when she had met Leon Stephanides, and a very young twenty at that. Although she had been working in Paris for three years as a model, her life had been almost as cloistered as that of a young novice. She lived with a family known to her employer—a family who guarded her as strictly as they might have done one of their own daughters—and after the exhaustion of a ten-hour day of modelling she had wanted to do nothing more in the evening that simply kick off her shoes and relax. Until Leon came into her life. Everything had changed then. She had responded to him like a tender young plant to the sun, expanding and unfurling in the warmth of his presence. How fatally easy she had made it all for him!

She had been delirious with joy when he proposed to her. Her parents had flown to Paris for the wedding—a huge affair, for Leon was the head of a Greek shipping empire. Her mother had suggested then that they might be rushing things, but Chloe had pushed her gentle warning aside. She loved Leon and he loved her. What a gullible fool she had been! Why on earth hadn't she stopped to think? Why hadn't she questioned why Leon, a wealthy, handsome Greek should look outside his own nationality for a wife? Why hadn't she asked why there had been no customary arranged marriage for him?

Because she had been besotted with love, that was why. That Leon, thirty, worldly, and experienced, to her naïve twenty-one, should actually love her had seemed so close to a miracle that she had not been able to question anything, least of all this lordly, almost god-like man whose cool lips teased her own into heated submission, whose lean fingers against her breast aroused such a turmoil of emotions that she was almost sick with wanting him. She who had never known passion was suddenly caught in its turbulent maelstrom.

Their honeymoon had been all she had dreamed of and more. Leon had taken her to the heights, had taught her unskilled body to recognise a deeply sensual core she had never known it possessed. The very texture of his skin beneath her fingers had been sufficient to turn her bones to water, her senses to mindless, feverish pleasure. Never once in the month they spent together on the Riviera had she doubted Leon's love. Never once had she questioned that as his wife hers was the most important place in his life. And how bitterly she had paid for those mistakes!

'Kyria!' Chloe was jolted out of the past by the breathless voice of one of the waiters who had obviously come looking for her. 'If you will please return to the hotel, the manager would speak with you,' the boy began respectfully as Chloe uncurled her slender limbs and got to her feet. Although her features were not regular enough for perfect classical beauty the fragility of her bone structure combined with the deep amethyst colour of her eyes and the pale fairness of her hair made people stop and take notice of her, and nowhere more so than in Greece, where her fair colouring drew constant glances of admiration from the Greek men.

'A sea nymph', was how Leon had once described her, with skin as translucent as the most perfect pearl and hair the colour of moonwashed sand, and she, like the gullible fool that she was, had been taken in by his meaningless flattery, never dreaming that it was all merely a façade to blind her to the truth—a truth so ugly that even now she could not bear to face up to it. Not even her parents knew the real reason she had left Leon. No one did. It was a bitter secret which would remain locked away in her heart until the day she died.

As she followed the waiter back to the hotel she tried to push aside her preoccupation with the past and concentrate instead on the situation she now found herself in. The manager greeted her with a smile which did much to banish the worst of her fears, and once again she was ushered into the luxurious office and invited to sit down.

'By the greatest of good fortune one of our most influential directors was at the Athens office when I telephoned there this morning,' he told Chloe. 'I explained to him the unfortunate circumstances you find yourself in and he has promised to do all he can to put matters right.'

Smiling gratefully, Chloe stood up. She could only hope that the manager's faith in his superior was not ill founded.

'For now you must just enjoy your holiday. As soon as I have more news you will be informed of it,' the manager told her with another smile.

Which was comforting, but in actual fact told her very little, Chloe reflected a little later alone in her

room. Her hotel expenses had been paid before she
left England, fortunately, and Thos was not large
enough to merit the need for large amounts of 'spending money'. Still, it was an uncomfortable feeling to
be alone in a foreign country with nothing more than
ten pounds in small change.

She was a little late going down for dinner and
found that most of the tables in the elegant dining
room were already occupied. A smiling waiter found
her a chair at a table with a pleasant middle-aged
couple from Surrey who were spending their second
holiday on Thos. Neither of them seemed to find
anything unusual in the fact that Chloe was apparently alone.

'Thos isn't large enough to warrant the hiring of a
car,' Richard Evans told Chloe over coffee, 'and like
most of these small islands it isn't really geared for
them—thank goodness. I sometimes envy these Greek
millionaires who buy themselves one of these tiny
islands. There's something about owning one's own
island that's very dear to the heart of most men—
especially Britons. It comes from being an island race,
I suppose.'

Chloe agreed with him. She could still remember
her own girlhood envy of Enid Blyton's tomboy heroine with her own small island domain.

One reminiscence led to another, and when the
manager suddenly appeared at her elbow Chloe was
astonished to realise how quickly the evening had
flown. She had been enjoying herself so much that
she had actually almost forgotten about her stolen
passport and travellers' cheques.

'Have you any news for me?' she asked the
manager, hoping against hope that Derek had come

to his senses and perhaps left her passport at the airport.

'You are to go to Athens,' he told her in reply. 'Everything is arranged. A helicopter is here to take you, and when you get there you will be met. . . .'

'Athens?' Chloe began to protest, remembering the lengthy sea journey from the port of Piraeus to Thos. 'But. . . .'

'It *is* necessary, *kyria*,' the manager assured her quickly. 'The loss of a passport is not to be treated lightly. There are documents to be completed, officials to see. . . .'

He was quite right, Chloe accepted resignedly, and her passport was not simply lost, but stolen. She gnawed at her lip, trying to estimate how long she would be in Athens and what she would need to take with her. Surely one change of clothes would be sufficient?

'You will spend the night at our sister hotel in Athens,' she was told, 'and then in the morning you will be taken to see the officials who deal with such matters.'

They were going to a lot of trouble on her behalf, Chloe thought, starting to thank him for his assistance. It was nothing, she was told with a beaming smile. If she would just pack whatever she needed for the brief stay in Athens, he would escort her to where the helicopter waited.

Chloe had never travelled in such a machine before, and said as much when, fifteen minutes later, she and the manager were walking across the tarmac-enclosed space at the rear of the hotel which she had not realised existed until this moment.

It was an enjoyable method of travelling, she was

assured, especially when time was short. 'The consortium which owns this hotel also owns others, and its executives frequently use company helicopters to travel from hotel to hotel.'

It would certainly save her a good deal of time, Chloe reflected. If she was lucky she could be back on Thos within twenty-four hours with all the tangles of her missing passport satisfactorily sorted out. While she was in Athens it might not be a bad idea to visit the British Embassy there, she decided, just to inform them of the position, although she would have to be careful what she said. She was furious with Derek, but she had no desire to brand him as a criminal.

The pilot of the helicopter gave her a cursory glance as she climbed into the machine. The noise of the rotating blades prevented conversation even if Chloe had wanted to talk, and within seconds they were airborne, rising above the hotel and out across the small bay where fishing boats were preparing to put out to sea, the lights from their mastheads reflected in the water like so many drowned stars.

Chloe had no clear idea of how long it would take to get to Athens. She knew they were passing over other islands by the glitter of lights far below them, but she could see nothing on the horizon remotely resembling the mainland of Greece itself.

When the helicopter suddenly started to lose height she was taken off guard, looking instinctively downward expecting to see the lights of Athens International Airport, but instead all she could see was one single solitary searchlight casting a blinding glare up into the purple-black night sky.

This was not Athens, she thought seconds later as the helicopter bumped down to earth. It couldn't possibly be. She glanced instinctively at the pilot, but he was already opening his door, turning away from her and into the darkness. A soft breeze blew in through the half open door, carrying with it the faint scent of thyme. In the distance Chloe could hear male voices speaking in Greek. Panic filled her and she pushed open her door, stepping blindly out into the darkness, and would have stumbled if a calloused male hand had not not grasped her arm.

'The *kyria* will come this way.'

The voice was curt but not unkind. Chloe opened her mouth to question where she was, and then closed it as she was propelled inexorably along a narrow path which seemed to lead upwards from the small plateau where the pilot had put the helicopter down. There was a moment when Chloe was able to pull back and turn round, but the powerful rotor blades of the machine were already turning faster and faster as the pilot prepared for take-off.

'Just what's going on?' she demanded huskily, trying not to let her fear show in her voice, but the man who was holding her arm made no response, merely reinforcing his grip and urging her more determinedly along the narrow path.

It ended abruptly on a patio illuminated by the lights blazing from the expanse of plate glass windows overlooking the gardens and the swimming pool beyond it. Despite the vivid illumination the house seemed deserted, and fear trickled down Chloe's spine like drops of iced water. Not normally given to febrile imaginings, all at once she felt her normal good sense deserting her completely, leaving her prey to clamouring fear.

'Where am I? Why have you brought me here?'

she demanded through lips almost too stiff to frame the words.

The house facing her was plainly not that of a poor man—long and low, what she could see of it, and the patio and the enormous swimming pool running alongside it spoke of luxury and wealth.

Someone moved against the brilliant backdrop of the illuminated rooms beyond the patio, a man's shadow, tall, broad-shouldered, moving with a menacing stealth gradually obliterated the light as he descended the small flight of steps set into the patio and walked towards them.

Chloe knew that her captor had relaxed his hold of her arm, but she couldn't have moved even if she had wanted to. The light from the house which masked the features of the man walking away from it revealed her own in stark detail, fear and dread written clearly in her eyes as he answered her questions in the cool drawl she remembered from what seemed like a lifetime ago when, unbelievably, merely to hear this man speak had sent her dizzy with nervous excitement.

'You're on Eos,' she was told calmly. 'Island of the Dawn. As to why—I think you know the answer to that, Chloe.'

He must have made some gesture she had missed, because her gaoler melted away, leaving them alone at the edge of the patio. As always Leon had made sure he had the advantage, Chloe thought bitterly, and not merely in bringing her here like this. Even the way he stood, with his back to the light, several inches above her, when he was already fully six inches taller than she, spoke of his determination to overwhelm her. But she was not the silly, gullible young fool who had married him any more. She was a woman, aware of so much that had been hidden from her then. She moved slightly so that Leon also was forced to move, the light from the house falling sharply on features which had not changed, but merely set harder as though hewn from a marble impervious to the elements. He had always been good-looking, but now, without the blinds of innocence which had hidden so much from her, Chloe saw the aggressive sexuality of his features; the bone structure which was entirely male; the high, taut cheekbones and the sensually curved mouth. He was wearing his hair longer than she remembered, and her fingers clenched involuntarily against the memory of its thick silky texture beneath her fingers. Only his eyelashes betrayed a hint of vulnerability—deceptively, as Chloe knew to her cost—for they were long and dark, almost theatrically so against the silvery grey eyes that were an inheritance from a distant ancestress—an Englishwoman said to have travelled to Greece seeking Lord Byron, but who instead had found Leon's ancestor and remained to bear his children.

'I *know* the answer?' Chloe's delicate eyebrows arched. She was drawing heavily on the experience she had gained since she left Leon; the ability to mask her true feelings which she now always wore like an invisible protective layer of clothing. She had no idea what Leon wanted, but there was simply no way she was going to let him see how his unexpected appearance had unnerved her. Nothing he could say or do could possibly affect her now, she reminded herself. The love she had once felt for him had been a girl's adolescent crush on a handsome, sexually experienced male, that was all. The man she had thought him to be; the man she had loved had never actually existed. Her lips twisted a little as she remembered how he had broken down all her barriers, turned her from a shy gauche child into a passionate woman, drawing from her a response she had never dreamed herself capable of giving. But it had all been a chimera, a selfishly and cold-bloodedly planned deception.

'You want a divorce?' She heard herself ask the question as calmly as though they were discussing nothing more important than the weather. She made herself pivot carelessly on one heel as though about to walk off in the opposite direction. 'My dear Leon, you can have one, and there was no need for this ridiculous charade.'

'I agree.' The soft voice had grown unexpectedly harsh, the faintly menacing quality of his body causing anxious tremors to flutter upwards along Chloe's tense nerves.

'But then I haven't gone to all this trouble because I want a divorce, Chloe.'

She moistened her lips, suddenly desperately afraid. Up until now events had possessed a vaguely dreamlike quality which had prevented her from fully experiencing the panic which was now sweeping through her, telling her that she must put as great a distance between this man and herself as she possibly could, but like Pandora she felt herself unable to stop herself from framing the question she knew Leon was silently willing her to ask.

'Then what do you want?'

'I want you, Chloe.' He said it so softly, she thought she must have misunderstood, but there was no misunderstanding his next words. 'I want you, because you are my wife. No Greek allows his wife's desertion of him to go unpunished, and your greatest punishment, I think, will be to be forced to return to the role you abandoned so precipitately—and publicly.'

Chloe blenched, turning desperately aside, but it was too late. Fingers like steel trapped her wrist, hauling her up against a chest which she could now see was rising and falling with the force of the rage pent up inside it.

'You little bitch, you really know where to hit where it hurts, don't you? But you're going to pay, Chloe. You should have remembered when you left me that I'm Greek, and Greeks never forget an insult—or forgive it.'

'I won't come back to you,' Chloe managed to get out. 'I won't!'

Leon's dark features seemed to swim above her in a dark mist, his lips contorted into a savagely bitter facsimile of a smile.

'Oh yes, you will,' he told her menacingly. 'And not only that, you'll give me a son to replace the one you destroyed.'

From a great distance Chloe heard a high-pitched, terrified protest as a great chasm of blackness opened up and engulfed her, and she fell down and down as though she were falling into the deepest pits of hell itself.

CHAPTER TWO

'MADAME is tired and must be left to sleep.'

It was several seconds before Chloe could place the faintly accented voice. At first she thought she was in Paris—Paris, where she had lived as a young girl and grown used to hearing her native tongue spoken with a faint French inflection, but then the hazy clouds of sleep parted and she remembered exactly where she was and why.

She sat bolt upright in a double bed which, huge though it was, made scarcely any impression at all in a room so large that it could easily have accommodated her tiny London flat twice over.

It was decorated in the softest greens and silver. Mermaid colours. She blenched as she realised where she had remembered those words from. It had been on her honeymoon: Leon had used them to describe a gown he had bought her in St Tropez. Leon. She closed her eyes, willing herself to stay calm, and when she opened them again a small plump woman was hovering anxiously at the side of the bed.

'The master said to let the *kyria* sleep. Gina,' she scolded the small girl standing behind her, holding a breakfast tray, 'you have disturbed Madame with all your noise!'

The girl looked ready to burst into tears, and Chloe shook her head, forcing a smile.

'No . . . no, it's quite all right. Just leave the tray.'

The events of the previous evening were beginning

to flood back, and she shuddered as she remembered the look on Leon's face as he told her that he meant to be revenged on her for publicly shaming him by leaving him, and not just that. She was glad that there was no one in the room to witness the way her hand trembled as she recalled the ferocity in Leon's voice when he told her that she would bear him a son—to replace the life she had destroyed, he had said. She pushed her tray aside, swinging her legs out of bed, stumbling across to the large curtained window. The life *she* had destroyed. Hysteria bubbled up inside her. Did he still think he could deceive her? And why the change of heart?

'Chloe?'

She whirled round, gasping with shock. She hadn't heard him enter her room. She would have given anything not to have to face him like this, disadvantaged by the flimsy nightdress she was wearing and the evidence of her fear written plainly in her eyes. He, in direct contrast, was wearing an immaculate business suit, his dark hair damp as though he had recently stepped out of the shower. A shuddering sensation of weakness swamped over her, her body traitorously reminding her of other occasions—occasions when she had shared his shower with him, taking sensual pleasure in the act. Panic flared suddenly and she turned round, her eyes darkening to misty purple as she pleaded with him.

'Let me go, Leon. You can't keep me here indefinitely—it isn't possible. Why are you doing this? I can't see any purpose in it.'

'Can't you? Then you must be incredibly thick-skulled. I thought I made my meaning more than plain last night.' He followed the flickering glance of her eyes to the large bed, and laughed mirthlessly. 'Last night was simply a respite. And besides, when I take you in my arms I want you to be very sure of what's happening to you, Chloe. You won't be allowed to escape me by fainting like some Victorian heroine.'

'You mean you expect me . . . you. . . .' Suddenly she couldn't speak for the huge lump in her throat. Oh, she knew that last night Leon had told her exactly why he had brought her to this island—an island which apparently was only inhabited by himself and his staff—but somehow she had never expected him to go through with it.

'You can't do this!' she protested wildly when he continued to look at her. 'You simply can't do it. It's against the law.'

'For a man to take possession of his wife?' he asked with deceptive suaveness. 'Not against Greek law, Chloe. In fact, many of my countrymen would think I have been decidedly forbearing. You run off and leave me; humiliate me in front of all my friends, encourage them to question how I can maintain control of a huge business empire if I cannot control one small woman, and then you tell me what I can and can't do? On Eos my word is law, Chloe, and by going to Thos you played straight into my hands. I had been wondering how to coax you back to Greece for some time—that you should choose to do so of your own free will was an unexpected bonus.'

A dreadful suspicion was beginning to take root in Chloe's mind. She stared across the room.

'You mean you. . . .'

'I arranged for your "friend" to desert you?' He laughed, the sound mirthless. 'You always were a poor judge of character, weren't you? His "friend-ship" proved surprisingly inexpensive. But don't worry, you won't miss him. Was he your only lover?'

It was on the tip of Chloe's tongue to tell him the truth, but she bit back the words, unwilling for Leon to know that since the break-up of their marriage there had been no one else. Even now she could scarcely take it in that Leon had actually planned for her to come to Eos, for Derek to desert her and for her to be brought here to this tiny island.

'I could have simply had you kidnapped in England, of course,' he drawled, accurately reading her mind. 'But this way is far less . . . complicated. You see, Chloe, when you left me, you did far more than simply break up our marriage. In Greece we take such things seriously, and for a woman to leave her husband casts a slur upon him that is not easily removed.'

'So what am I supposed to do? Tell everyone that I didn't mean it and that you're really Mr Wonderful?' Her lip curled. 'You've overreached yourself, Leon. The moment you let me leave this island I'll leave you again, and if you keep me in-carcerated here no one is going to believe the fallacy that we're reunited.' She lifted her head and stared proudly at him. 'The only way I would conceive your child would be if you forced yourself upon me— I'm talking about rape, Leon, because that is what it would be. I don't want you, and I don't want your child!'

'Why, you. . . .'

For a moment Chloe thought he was going to hit her, but the hand he had raised dropped to his side, only the muscle working in his jaw betraying the

savagery of the emotions she had aroused. Chloe
wanted to look away, but something prevented her.
Sickness clawed at her stomach, all that she had
fought to suppress for so long rising to the surface,
making her shudder with remembered revulsion.

Leon came towards her, his fingers bruising the
tender flesh of her arms as he wrenched her round
into the light, his glance travelling slowly over her
body, stripping from it the brief protection of her
nightgown.

'Last night my servants undressed you and put you
to bed. They know nothing of our relationship except
that we have been separated and are now together.
Tonight and for as many nights as it takes until you
carry my child we will share this room and this bed. I
have your passport, Chloe, and without that you are
virtually my prisoner whether we remain on this
island or live in the middle of Athens.'

It was true, so true that Chloe sobbed out bitterly,
'And Marisa—where does she fit into all this? Does
she have no say in the matter? About your plans to
become a father? Or have you forgotten that she
destroyed our first child?'

This time he did hit her. Shock rather than pain
made her reel, her eyes widening. Above her Leon's
face was nearly as pale as her own, the bones standing
out sharply.

'You will never say that again,' he said thickly.
'Do you understand me? Never! Marisa. . . .'

He never finished what he was going to say, for the
door swung open and a young Greek girl burst impetuously in, her eyes hardening as she saw Chloe.

'What's she doing here?' she spat viciously. 'Leon,
you. . . .'

Her long fingernails were painted dark red to match the glossy lipstick emphasising the sullen pout of a mouth curved with sensual promise.

Three years ago, when Leon had mentioned to her his half-sister for whom he was responsible, Chloe had visualised a shy, gawky teenager—a girl with whom she could be friends; a girl who might perhaps need her guidance and affection, but Marisa needed nothing from her brother's wife, unless it was the protection of her presence to deceive the world as Chloe herself had once been deceived. Her hands went to her stomach in unthinking protection long before she remembered that there was now no vulnerable life there for her to protect.

Marisa's eyes followed the gesture, narrowing with bitter fury as she rounded on Leon.

'What is she doing here? Why. . . .'

The arm he had slid round Chloe's waist felt like a steel hawser. She tried to pull away. She could feel the warmth of his breath against her hair, but she deliberately turned away from it, sickened by the falsity of the tableau. It was plain that Marisa knew nothing about her own presence here on Eos, and Chloe could only surmise that Leon was insisting on the resumption of their marriage to protect the younger girl. Not that Marisa herself cared the slightest about public opinion. She would have lived openly with Leon. She had told Chloe as much. It was Leon who had insisted that they must observe the conventions. Leon who had decided to find himself a quiet, biddable wife, too naïve to see what was happening under her eyes. And she had been that wife. Until Marisa, in a fit of jealousy had opened her eyes to the truth.

'Why? Because it is necessary.'

When Leon spoke in that tone even Marisa did not dare to argue. Chloe could see the baffled rage in her eyes and wondered if perhaps Leon was subtly punishing the Greek girl. Her suspicions were reinforced when Leon's free hand cupped *her* jaw, forcing her head round in a grip that looked casual, but which in actual fact was anything but. Her bones ached from the pressure of his hold. 'Isn't it, Chloe?'

He whispered the question a hair's breadth from her lips in a gesture deliberately sensual. She tried not to succumb to it, but it was there in her eyes and the sudden tensing of her muscles, betraying her far more effectively than any words, and she knew from the sudden alert gleam in Leon's eyes that he knew she was aware of him. It seemed to Chloe, her senses heightened by the emotional violence in the air of the room, that he was holding her more closely than he had been doing; that he was deliberately moulding her body to his in a way he hadn't been doing before, so that she was intimately aware of him. It had been like this the first time they met. Leon had come to a viewing. She had been modelling an evening gown, had looked up and seen him, and it had been as though he had reached out and touched her. In the years they had been apart she had convinced herself that now she was immune to that sort of deliberate sexual arousal, but now, with his fingers tracing her spine, his body making her aware of the fact that physically she still aroused him, Chloe knew that she was still desperately vulnerable.

She closed her eyes, swallowing painfully, and when she opened them again Leon was watching her like a cat at a mousehole. For a second she thought

he was going to kiss her, and moistened her lips instinctively, trembling convulsively as his free hand
pushed her hair behind her ears. Was he remembering, as she was, how he had woken her in the mornings
of their honeymoon with teasing kisses placed in the
soft hollows behind her ears, tracing a path along the
vulnerable line of her throat, down to her breasts
when, inevitably, her fingers would curl into the thick
darkness of his hair, urging him against the flesh he
had aroused so thoroughly?

No, she mustn't think about that! About how she
had felt; how she had ached for his possession. She
must remember afterwards, when she had learned
about Marisa.

The slamming of her bedroom door brought her
back to earth. Marisa had gone and they were alone.
Leon released her coolly, his glance mockingly aware
of the response he had drawn from her.

'You are still my wife, Chloe,' he reminded her.
'And in Greece a man's wife is still his possession, to
do with as he wishes.'

'And we both know what you wish to do with me,'
Chloe said bitterly. 'Impregnate me with your child.
Why, Leon?'

He shrugged. 'All men want sons, do they not? It is
a law of nature. I am a rich man and must have heirs
of my body to follow after me. You are my wife. . . .'

'Oh, for Pete's sake stop saying that! We both
know why I'm your wife; *why* you married me. . . .'

Before Leon could reply, the same man who had
escorted her from the helicopter the previous evening
knocked on the door, which Leon had started to open.
Leon moved immediately, shielding Chloe with the
bulk of his body, as the other man, who was appar-

ently his personal assistant, explained that there was a call from New York.

'Don't try to leave,' Leon warned Chloe before he left, 'because you can't. Even if you managed to leave this island—which you could only do by swimming— I still have your passport.'

What on earth the staff must make of the situation she dared not think, Chloe reflected ten minutes later, standing under the needle-sharp spray of the shower in the bathroom which led off her bedroom. Decorated in the same colours as the bedroom, it had a huge round bath, sunk into the floor and surrounded by soft green marble tiles. As Chloe reached for one of the soft silver-grey towels she caught sight of her naked body in the mirror-lined wall. Already faint bruises were beginning to form where Leon had gripped her. Even now she could not believe that she was actually here on Eos, Leon's prisoner. Her eyes went instinctively to the open bathroom door and the bed beyond it. Leon had talked about them sharing it as matter-of-factly as though they were two strangers contemplating sharing a taxi. A frisson of awareness shivered through her as she remembered how she had felt in his arms. By rights she ought to feel indifference if not outright hatred, but while her mind might reject and be repulsed by Leon's cynical attitude her body could still be physically aroused by him.

A woman never forgot her first lover. Chloe shivered as she remembered reading that somewhere. It was true; almost as though Leon's touch was a secret code to which her body would always respond.

Dressed in the change of clothes she had expected to be wearing in Athens, Chloe tried to reason with

herself. She was not a mindless machine. There was
such a thing as free will. Surely her mind was capable
of overcoming her body's weakness? Of course it was.
Hadn't she proved that during these last two years?
Abstinence was easy without temptation, a tiny inner
voice warned her, but Chloe refused to heed it. The
love she had once thought she felt for Leon had died,
and the emotions she was now experiencing were
merely reaction to his sudden eruption into her life.

Unbidden, the memory of Leon's expression when
he told her that he wanted from her the child she had
previously denied him surfaced, and she shivered
despite the heat. How could Leon have accused her
of that? Her mouth twisted. Perhaps it was just another example of his warped way of thinking. A man
who was capable of seducing his young half-sister
and then marrying someone else purely to provide a
cover for their affair was surely capable of anything.
And yet Chloe could have sworn that for a moment
there had been actual pain in his voice when he
spoke of the child she was to have borne; the child
Marisa had destroyed in a fit of jealous rage, but then
Leon had always refused to believe that Marisa had
been responsible for her fall. During the early months
of their marriage—before she learned the truth—
Chloe had never been able to understand how a man
as intelligent as Leon could so readily accept
Marisa's lies; and there had been many of them. Not
important on the surface perhaps, but hurtful and
barbed, intentionally aimed at putting Chloe in a
bad light. But then of course she had not realised that
Marisa viewed her not in the light of an older sister-
in-law but with all the intense jealousy of a rival for
the attentions of the man she loved. And of course

Marisa had the advantage of having a double claim on Leon—as his half-sister and as his mistress.

Chloe pulled a wry face. Mistress! How old-fashioned it sounded; how full of connotations no longer considered important by sophisticates. But some shibboleths still held as strong a sway on people's emotions as they had always done, and incest was one of the few remaining taboos. By Greek standards Leon had committed the unforgivable sin. In Greek eyes there was no greater responsibility than that owed by a man to his sisters. By rights Marisa should have been married long before now. She was, after all, twenty-two. But then Marisa would never marry. She had told Chloe that herself, the day she had told her so much, including the fact that she and Leon were lovers and had been for several years.

'Chloe!'

She hadn't heard Leon enter the room. In addition to completing his telephone call he had changed his clothes and was now wearing jeans and a thin cotton shirt which clung to the powerful muscles of his shoulders. Pain as sharp as a splinter of ice entering her heart lanced through Chloe. So had he dressed during those all too brief weeks of their honeymoon when she had still believed that she was the one who he loved; when her own fears had been that she, with her innocence and sheltered upbringing, would prove to be an unworthy companion of so sophisticated and experienced a man.

She remembered how, when she had tried to put her doubts into words, Leon had silenced her with drugging kisses. Her innocence only endeared her to him all the more, he had told her in the husky voice that never failed to thrill her. All that she needed to learn she would learn from him. As Marisa had learned!

'What do you want, Leon?' The words sounded sharply shrill—defensive, and Chloe regretted them instantly. Anger flared smokily in Leon's eyes and she knew that she had annoyed him. Even in those early days she had recognised that Leon was a man of strong will. When she had remonstrated with him, saying that they had hardly known one another long enough to talk about marriage, he had simply crushed her objections beneath the warmth of his lips, over-riding her fears by arousing her emotions to such a pitch that she could deny him nothing. And he had known it. How he must have laughed at her! Thoughts which she had never allowed herself to examine properly before refused to be banished any longer, and Chloe writhed inwardly in recognition of how easy she had made it for Leon. She hadn't even had the wit to try and hide from him how she felt. He could have seduced her as easily as he had no doubt seduced Marisa and she wouldn't have raised the slightest objection. Perhaps it would have better had he done so. An affair was easier to leave behind than a marriage.

'You know what I want—a son to replace the one you destroyed. And you will give me one, Chloe.'

'And Marisa—does she know of this sudden compulsive desire? I know how you feel about her, Leon, and how she feels about you. What are you planning to do? Divorce me once I've borne this son you want so badly?'

'I *was* intending to fly to Athens this morning,' Leon commented, changing the subject. 'But my appointment has been cancelled, so I shall show you round the villa instead. My meeting was an important one, but my associate understood that it would not be possible for me to visit his office, having been so recently reunited with my wife.'

The words held a subtle threat, but Chloe refused to acknowledge it, or to look upwards at Leon who she knew was watching her.

'As my wife you will now have to take up certain responsibilities. We shall be expected to do a certain amount of entertaining, so it is as well that you familiarise yourself with the layout of the villa.'

Entertaining! Now Chloe did look at him. In the tanned harshness of his face, his eyes stood out like sharp pieces of flint.

'You would take such a risk? I'm not a child to be ordered about any more, Leon—you no longer hold me in thrall. I've grown up. You might be able to hold me on this island against my will, but you can't stop me telling your friends what you're doing. Once before you used me—you're not going to do it a second time.'

Chloe could tell by his expression that she had hit home, but the anger she could see burning behind the watchful glitter of his eyes was quickly masked, his voice cool with malice as he drawled softly, 'Go ahead and tell them—they won't care. In Greece a man's wife is his property to do with as he wishes. They will laugh at you, Chloe, if you dare to complain—laugh and praise me for treating you as an errant wife should be treated. Indeed, many of them will think your punishment extremely light. Greek men do not have Western scruples about striking women. Oh, it's all right,' he sneered when Chloe flinched back. 'Physical domination holds no appeal for me.'

His open mockery made Chloe clench her fists at her sides. 'You dare to say that?' she stormed bitterly. 'When not five minutes ago you were telling me that you were going to force your child upon me. . . .'

'Force?' His gaze sharpened, narrowing on the betraying rise and fall of her breasts beneath the fine lawn of her blouse. 'You keep using that word, but I seem to recall that "force" was never necessary between us, Chloe—far from it.' As he spoke his fingers reached for her wrist, circling it, his thumb lazily stroking the tender inner flesh with sensual expertise. 'Well?'

Her mouth dry, Chloe tried to find the words to deny his mocking assertion, but Leon was already drawing her close to him, his free hand pulling her cotton blouse from the waistband of the matching patterned skirt she was wearing with it.

Her muscles clenched in protest as his fingers traced the sensitive bones of her spine, reaching upwards to slip under the brief lacy bra she was wearing before she could take evasive action.

'Leon!' Her sharp protest was smothered by her own shocked gasp as his hand slid forward to cup the warm fullness of her breast.

'Is this what you call force, Chloe?' he demanded softly, his lean, experienced fingers stroking and teasing her nipple until awareness of its burgeoning hardness washed over her body in a heated wave.

'Stop it. Stop it!' She lifted her hands to push him away, but all her action did was to lift and tauten her breasts until they were clearly defined beneath the thin cotton—and with them her obvious arousal.

Damn Leon, she thought impotently, not daring to

lift her eyes for fear of the open mockery she would see in his. What duplicity men were capable of! Leon loved Marisa, and yet here he was fully intent on and capable of making love to her!

'I won't do it, Leon,' she said in distaste. 'I won't be forced into despising myself—into giving you a child to satisfy some primitive paternalistic urge. You might be able to arouse me physically, but. . . .'

'But you hate yourself for allowing it to happen?' Leon jeered. 'What happened to the girl I married, Chloe? The girl who gave herself to me so willingly; who revelled in my possession of her body?'

'She doesn't exist any more,' Chloe said tonelessly, refusing to allow his words to affect her.

'No?'

She saw the ugly look in his eyes too late to prevent him from ruthlessly plundering her mouth with a force that ground her lips against her teeth, bruising the tender flesh as she struggled to free herself. For the first time in her life Chloe experienced the degradation of a kiss designed to inflict pain instead of pleasure, to enforce and go on enforcing man's ability to physically dominate woman, and turn what should have been a mutually pleasurable experience into sexual punishment.

'If it's force you want then force you shall have,' Leon ground out as he released her abruptly. 'Now, shall I show you round the villa, or would you prefer us to remain here—where I can reinforce my intentions of getting from you a replacement for the child you destroyed?'

She destroyed, Chloe thought numbly as she inched past him into the corridor. Was he even now going to go on with that ridiculous charade?

Her lips felt swollen and sore, but she daren't touch them for fear of drawing Leon's attention to her. When he reached towards her she flinched away, shrinking beneath the anger she saw blazing in his eyes momentarily before he shrugged with a non-chalance she couldn't help envying.

'I'm not about to rape you in the corridor,' he drawled sardonically. 'But unless you want the entire household to suspect I've just been making love to you, it might be as well if you did something about that.'

Lean fingers flicked disparagingly at the cotton blouse, which she had forgotten was hanging betrayingly over her skirt, as he spoke. Keeping as far away from him as possible, Chloe tucked it back into her waistband, hating the betraying way her fingers trembled, and the knowing gleam in Leon's eyes as they rested on the soft thrust of her breasts beneath the thin fabric. Overriding every emotion was an intense desire to prove to Leon that she was immune to whatever sexual enticement or harassment he might choose to exert, but at the back of her mind Chloe acknowledged that her feelings mattered little to him. They couldn't do. If they did he would never have brought her here like this and for such a purpose.

True to his word, Leon insisted on showing her over the villa. It was huge—far larger than she had first imagined, and equipped with every modern appliance and device conceivable, all fuelled by the generator housed away from the main building. An advanced security system protected the island, a necessary precaution in these days, Leon pointed out when she commented on it, especially in view of his known wealth. While acknowledging that he spoke no less than the truth, Chloe couldn't help feeling that he had a secondary motive in showing her the complex security precautions—it was as though he were subtly reinforcing his earlier claim that there was no way in which she could leave the island without him knowing. Chloe now acknowledged that this was true. Sophisticated technological advances meant that it was possible for an effective guard to be placed over the island while at the same time maintaining its privacy. Electronic eyes could see far more than human ones, and far less obtrusively!

The only form of transport on and off the island was Leon's own private helicopter, and apart from the occupants of the villa it was completely uninhabited. It was too small to support a population, Leon told her—too small and too barren, but among the rocky cliffs were small sandy beaches which made it a holiday paradise when combined with the heat of the Aegean sun and the silky waters of its sea.

The villa had apparently been built to Leon's specific design, and as she was shown from room to room Chloe was overwhelmed by a sense of familiarity, and then at last, standing in the huge living room with its elegant Italian furniture, she realised why. It was almost an exact replica of a villa they had visited during their honeymoon. It had belonged to a wealthy recluse and some friends of Leon's had been renting it. To Chloe it had seemed the epitome of elegance, and although Leon's villa was larger, she could see now that it was built on very similar lines, even down to the Italian furniture which she had so admired. She touched the pale cream silk settee, stroking the fine fabric, her eyes drawn to the jewel-bright colours of the silk scatter cushions carelessly heaped on to it. Chrome and glass shelving lined one wall, a modern marble fireplace in the same cream as the upholstery dominating another wall. Apart from the brilliant splashes of colour provided by the cushions and several carefully chosen objets d'art the entire room was decorated in the same pale cream as the furniture, the brilliant jades and greens of the cushions now chosen, Chloe realised, to complement the collection of jade housed in one of the chrome wall units.

'Recognise it?' Leon mocked. 'I commissioned the same architect who designed the one in Antibes. It was going to be a present to mark our first anniversary.'

For a moment Chloe felt her defences weakening, but then she remembered how well Leon played his self-appointed role, and she forced herself to raise her eyebrows and say lightly,

'Really? I'm surprised you kept it. I should have thought it would hold too many unpleasant memories.'

'You know what they say about revenge,' Leon said softly. 'It needs feeding, and living here, always being reminded of why I commissioned it in the first place, helped to feed mine.'

He made it sound as though she were the one at fault; as though she were the one responsible for the break up of their marriage—a marriage which was really no marriage at all.

'Stop play-acting, Leon,' she demanded brittlely. 'There's no point.'

He turned to make some reply, but before he could speak, Marisa erupted into the room, her eyes blazing in her chalk white face.

'Leon,' she demanded, totally ignoring Chloe's presence, 'Gina has just told me that you have instructed her to prepare a suite for the Kriticos'. She says they are bringing Nikos with them. I will not have it, do you hear? I will not have him here. I will not be forced into a marriage simply so that you can have an heir. You cannot get rid of me so easily. . . .' She turned on Chloe. 'That's all he wants you for, you know; to provide him with a son, an heir for his business empire. But I will not marry Nikos. I'll die first!' She burst into noisy sobs, while Leon looked on impassively.

'I won't marry him, Leon,' she reiterated. 'I won't do it. You can't make me!'

'You are overwrought. We will discuss this entire matter later—although you already know my views on the subject.'

'I know that you want to get rid of me so that you can make a baby with her!' Marisa spat out, glaring at Chloe. 'Well, I won't let you! You belong to me, Leon . . . I won't let you! I . . . .'

Chloe turned away, filled with sickness and pity, unable to bear to watch Leon scooping the slender body into his arms or to listen to Marisa's hysterical pleas as he carried her out of the room.

If she had wanted proof of exactly how far Leon was prepared to go in his determination to have a son she had just received it. She knew she ought to feel triumph—now Marisa was experiencing the same pain and despair she had once known—but all she could feel towards the other girl was pity. She knew it was the established rule in Greek households for male relatives to find husbands for their female dependents, especially in the wealthier families where marriage partners had to be chosen with care, but she had never dreamed that Leon would exercise this right over Marisa!

She didn't wait for him to return to the salon, instead retreating to her bedroom, where once again her eyes were drawn to the enormous double bed. Was Leon really intending to share that bed with her? She looked at the bedroom door, searching in vain for a lock. There had been something implacable in his words which warned her against trying to plead with him, and besides, her pride would not allow her to stoop to such depths. So what was she to do? Endure his lovemaking and hope that she would conceive quickly? Never! There must be some way she could escape from Eos. There had to be!

CHAPTER THREE

CHLOE hadn't intended going down for dinner, but it struck her that Leon might come looking for her and take her non-appearance as mute acceptance of his wishes. Her skirt and blouse, apart from having been worn all day, were hardly suitable wear for dinner, but they were all she had with her.

She stepped out of the shower and froze as she realised that there was someone in the bedroom beyond, but it was not Leon who appeared in the open doorway. It was the young maid who had brought her breakfast.

'Which dress does the *kyria* wish me to lay out for tonight?' she asked hesitantly.

Chloe sighed, acknowledging that her Greek did not extend to explaining that her wardrobe was restricted to one cotton skirt and blouse and a pair of jeans and a tee-shirt.

'I have no clothes. . . .' she began slowly, but the girl dismissed her words with a triumphant flourish, pulling open the mirrored doors of the huge wardrobe running the entire length of one wall.

'Many, many clothes,' she protested enthusiastically. 'The *kyrios* had them brought from Athens in readiness.'

Chloe blinked and stared disbelievingly at the overflowing cupboards. When Leon planned something he didn't miss a single detail. She walked slowly across to the wardrobe, absently fingering a misty lilac dress in pure silk, which shrieked couture design, wondering how long Leon had been planning to force her to return to him.

'I ordered them from René. After all, he made your trousseau.' Leon had entered the room without her being aware of it. 'He still has your measurements,' he added casually.

Which had altered since the days when she had modelled for him, Chloe thought wryly, but she could see that the clothes were the right size—someone, either René or Leon himself, had realised that a woman of twenty-two was a different shape from a girl of eighteen, and had different tastes. These gowns were far more sophisticated than anything she had ever worn before! And far more expensive. Each one would have cost her several months' salary, and yet Leon dismissed them as though they were nothing.

'Not exactly sackcloth and ashes,' Leon mocked, watching the way she studied the clothes.

'They might as well be.' Chloe shut the wardrobe doors dismissively. 'You might have brought me to your island, Leon; you might be able to force me to stay here, and even ultimately to bear your child— that is if you don't mind descending to rape—but you can't force me to wear those clothes.'

'You think not?' He advanced on her with a grim implacability. The young maid had made a discreet disappearance the moment Leon entered the room and, despite its size, Chloe was overcome by a para-lysing sense of claustrophobia, engendered chiefly by the powerful bulk of Leon's body.

Afterwards she was to curse herself for her stupid-ity, but acting instinctively, she moved backwards, stopping only when her flight was impeded by the bed.

The towel she had wrapped sarong-wise around her slender body offered scant protection against the sensual scrutiny of pale grey eyes as they slid dangerously over smooth, pale shoulders, resting momentarily on the soft swell of her breasts before dropping lower to examine the rest of her body in a manner which brought a furious wave of colour to Chloe's skin.

'Stop it, Leon,' she demanded huskily. They both of them knew that whatever desire he felt towards her was purely a male physical response to a female body—any female body, and yet for a second, with his eyes lingering purposefully on the frail barrier of her towel, Chloe had experienced an almost overwhelming surge of desire so strong that if he had opened his arms she could not have prevented herself from running into them.

That knowledge lent determination to her voice and eyes as she reiterated her refusal to wear the clothes Leon had bought for her, her head held high as she tried to ignore the almost magnetic force of Leon's personality. She could almost feel the air pulsing with the sexual excitement his presence invoked—something she had forgotten in the time they had been apart, or was it simply that then she had been too naïve to recognise the tension between them for what it actually was? She could almost smell it in the air, taste it on her tongue, bitter-sweet and addictive—like Leon's lovemaking!

Stop it! she warned herself, her lips curling in fastidious distaste as she reminded herself that for Leon, making love to her was an act of war; the first step towards his revenge.

'You have two choices, Chloe,' he told her evenly, ignoring her command to leave. 'Either you wear those clothes willingly, or I will dress you in them myself. Be careful if you opt for the latter choice,' he added, his own mouth curving downward in sardonic mockery. 'I might interpret it as a desire to feel my hands on your body once more.'

'I'd rather die!' Chloe shot out hotly before she could stop herself, furious colour flooding her cheeks as she remembered how only seconds before she had almost been on the point of surrendering to his sexual magnetism.

'Liar! I could take you now—make you want to have me take you, and we both know it. Deny it as much as you like, you can't hide it from me, Chloe. You might hate me with your mind, but your body. . . .' The way he looked at her body, so explicitly meaningful, filled her with rage and pain. 'Your body would betray you if you allowed it to, Chloe. . . .'

'Never!'

'No? Are you asking me to prove you a liar? Is this a subtle way of indicating your desire? I'm sorry, but on this occasion I must disappoint you. My cook has prepared a special meal to celebrate our reunion. Perhaps later. . . .'

'You're wrong—I don't want you!' Chloe flung after his departing back. 'And there won't be any later!'

She meant it, every word of it. So why was there this curious ache in the pit of her stomach; this restless, driving core of energy that wouldn't let her relax? All the time she had been away from Leon she had not had the slightest desire to take a lover, and yet now, within hours of seeing him again, her mind and body were filled with aching memories of their love-making.

When he had gone she stared at the closed wardrobe, worrying the soft, full curve of her bottom lip with small white teeth. Almost it would be worthwhile going down to dinner in her jeans and tee-shirt just to see his face, but then she remembered what interpretation he had said he would put on such defiance, and her fingers reached mechanically for the door handle.

Almost automatically her hand came to rest on a gauzy chiffon dress in soft lilacs and lavenders. It might have been made for her, she acknowledged, holding it up in front of her. Putting it on, though, proved more difficult than she had anticipated. She had no problem with the long full sleeves gathered into a tight wristband and fastening with a tiny pearl button, nor with the matching buttons at the back of her neck. It was those farther down, below the edge of the delicately pleated collar and down to the waist, which defeated all her gyrations, and in the end Chloe was forced to concede defeat.

Arguing that it was better to finish dressing and then go in search of someone to help her, she slipped on the satin sandals obviously designed to go with the dress, and carefully applied some of the make-up she had discovered in one of the drawers in the bathroom. A misty lilac eyeshadow enhanced the colour of her eyes, a brief coat of mascara darkening the sun-bleached tips of her lashes. The skirt of her dress drifted in swirling panels to just below her knees—an elegant length, Monsieur René had always maintained, and Chloe agreed with him.

When she stepped into the corridor it was deserted—a disappointment, because she had been hoping to see one of the maids. Now she would have to go in search of someone to help her. A door to the right of her own opened and Leon strode out, impressively immaculate in a soft silk shirt and narrow dark trousers.

'You chose that one—good.'

Tempted by the satisfaction in his voice to rip the gown off her back, Chloe ignored him.

'You're a few minutes early,' Leon commented, unperturbed. 'Dinner is not usually served until eight, but if you wish we have a drink first. . . .'

'No, thank you. Actually I was looking for someone to help me with my dress,' Chloe defended unwisely. 'I couldn't manage all the buttons.'

'Allow me. Isn't that, after all, what husbands are for?' Leon asked mockingly.

There was no way Chloe could avoid his adroit fingers. While she stiffened her muscles in angry protest and waited for him to finish she heard another door open, and then the angry tip-tap of high heels along the tiled floor.

'Leon!'

Even to Chloe's ears Marisa's voice sounded shrill. One look confirmed that the Greek girl was in a furious temper—nothing new to Chloe, she had experienced too many of Marisa's temper tantrums in the past to be surprised by them now, but she had noticed how careful Marisa always was to hide the worst of her emotional thunderstorms from Leon.

Perhaps she now felt sure enough of him not to care, Chloe reflected, as Marisa ignored her, her brown eyes glittering feverishly as she turned to Leon.

'I won't do it, do you hear me? I won't marry anyone! If you try to force me I'll tell them the truth. I'll. . . .'

'You will do nothing,' Leon corrected in a far firmer voice than Chloe had ever heard him use to the younger girl before. 'We have discussed this at great length already, Marisa, and I shall not change my mind.'

'You just want to get rid of me!' Marisa accused, tearful now where she had been angry. 'You just want me out of the way, because of her! He doesn't care about *you*,' she flung at Chloe. 'All he wants is a son. Any son, as long as the father's him. It just so happens that being his wife makes you the natural choice.'

'Marisa!'

This time there was a distinct warning in the cold tones. 'I shall only say this one more time. When my friends arrive tomorrow with Nikos you will conduct yourself properly. This applies to both of you,' he added, turning to Chloe.

'And if I refuse? If I tell them why you're reunited with your wife, and how?' Marisa demanded.

'Then,' Leon replied cruelly, 'I shall tell them simply that you are a jealous child!'

'Was that absolutely necessary?' Chloe asked in a shaky voice minutes later when the sound of Marisa's slammed bedroom door still reverberated in the corridor.

'It is time that Marisa learned that if she insists on behaving like a child, she will be treated as one. However, what happens between my sister and myself need not concern you. I find your apparent sympathy

for her curious—in the circumstances, and bearing in
mind the accusations you have heaped upon her
head.'

'Do you?' Chloe muttered bitterly. She wasn't
going to explain that her sympathy for Marisa was
simply of that of one woman who had experienced
intense pain for another woman hurt by the same
man. Leon had been unnecessarily cruel, she
thought.

They dined in a heavy silence, broken only by the
soft-footed entry and exit of the servants. Chloe made
a pretence of eating, more for their sakes than Leon's,
but if someone had asked her what she was eating she
doubted that she could have answered properly.

After dinner Leon insisted on joining her to drink
his coffee. 'I meant what I said to Marisa,' he said
abruptly at one point. 'I shall expect you to play the
part of my newly reunited wife to the full, Chloe.'

'And if I find the role too taxing?' she enquired
sweetly.

'In that case we must ensure that you get sufficient
coaching, mustn't we? Actions, after all, speak louder
than words. As I recall, your eyes are most expressive,
my love. I well remember how they looked after a
night in my arms. That, I think, should suffice to
convince my guests!'

Ten minutes later, her coffee cup empty, Chloe
made her excuses and got up, declining Leon's suggestion that she stroll round the gardens with him.

'Why?' she demanded flippantly. 'So that you can
show me yet again the excellence of your defence
system? Thanks, but no, thanks. I'm already convinced.'

'Perhaps it is not so much the strength of my

defences you fear, but the weakness of your own, mm?' Leon challenged softly, his mocking laughter lingering in her ears long after she had left the drawing room behind her and exchanged it for the privacy of her own bedroom.

Not that she was allowed to enjoy that privacy for very long. She had barely stepped out of her dress, this time managing all the tiny buttons, and into the cream silk negligé Gina had left on the bed for her, than her door was thrust open with a bang loud enough to wake the dead.

'Preparing yourself for Leon, are you?' Marisa demanded angrily, her eyes on the cream silk. 'He doesn't really want you, you know. All he wants is a son. *You're* just the means of getting one.'

'So you've already said,' Chloe agreed dryly, surprised to see how easily she was holding on to her own temper. Before Marisa had always seemed to hold the upper hand, always been able to panic her into rash retaliation which she afterwards regretted. Perhaps it was merely that now she had nothing to lose, Chloe reflected, but whatever the reason, she was glad to be able to turn and face the other girl calmly, and even had time to feel sorry for her as she took in the tear-streaked cheeks and tumbled hair.

'You know why he's forcing me into this marriage, don't you?' Marisa hissed. 'He's obsessed with this desire for a son. Nothing else matters. Not me, not his business affairs, and especially not you. But it won't always be like this. When you've given him his son everything will change, you will see.'

'It needn't be like that,' Chloe said slowly, an idea suddenly coming to her. 'Help me to leave this island, Marisa. You can't want me here.'

'I don't,' the other girl admitted frankly, fear suddenly replacing hatred, and she gnawed at her bottom lip. 'But there's no way you could leave without Leon knowing. He won't let you go until you've given him a child. . . .'

'To replace the one he believes I deliberately destroyed,' Chloe said evenly. 'But we both know that wasn't true, don't we, Marisa? You destroyed my child, you pushed me down those steps. . . .'

Chloe sighed as yet again her bedroom door was slammed. She should have known better than to expect Marisa to admit to the truth. And that was the truth. Marisa had quite deliberately pushed her down those steps.

She walked over to the dressing table and started to brush her hair with long, rhythmic strokes, the action soothing, her thoughts winging back to the past.

She had been nervous of meeting Marisa, of course—as Leon's closest living relative she held an important place in his life, and during the flight from Paris to Athens Chloe had plagued Leon with questions about her.

He had answered her in monosyllables and she had thought his reticence was caused by tiredness— he had had business to complete in Paris before they left for Greece where he had an apartment. All she had known about Marisa before meeting her was that the Greek girl was the child of Leon's father's second marriage. Thirteen years younger than Leon, she had been in his sole care ever since the death of her parents. Her upbringing had been more modern than that permitted to most wealthy Greek girls. For one thing, she had been educated abroad—in

England and then Switzerland—and could have gone on to university had she shown any wish to do so.

She had been waiting for them in the apartment—and Chloe, overwhelmed by the sheer magnificence of the entrance hall and drawing room of her new home with its priceless antique furniture and beautiful Oriental rugs, had been able to do little more than register a certain coolness in Marisa's welcome.

As the days went by the coolness grew worse—always more marked when Leon was absent on business—until Chloe could not ignore it any longer. By this time she was sure that she was carrying Leon's child but had kept the news from him, wanting there to be no doubts before she told him.

He had been in Paris for a week. She could remember quite clearly how much she had missed him. How thrilled she had been to receive the note from the doctor she had been seeing, confirming that she was carrying Leon's child. Marisa had been even more difficult than usual, critical and sarcastic about Chloe's unfamiliarity with the things she herself took so much for granted—like walking into an exclusive boutique and calmly ordering whatever caught her eye without even bothering to check the price.

'Only parvenues need to do that,' she had sneered on one occasion when Chloe had insisted on knowing the price of a velvet evening gown before buying it.

Now such rudeness wouldn't worry her the slightest little bit, Chloe reflected, but then she had been so deeply insecure, so desperate to gain Marisa's approval, almost as though already she suspected the truth but was trying to blind herself to it; trying to convince herself that there was nothing unhealthily obsessive about the possessive manner in which

Marisa regarded her half-brother.

Chloe remembered that she had been anxious enough to mention her unease to Leon once or twice before he left for Paris, but on both occasions he had brushed aside her anxious words, shrugging and telling her that she was imagining things, taking her in his arms and making Marisa, and every other person in the universe apart from themselves, fade into insignificance beneath the pleasure of his lovemaking. If she hadn't been so naïve, so much in love, she might have suspected then from Leon's very unwillingness to talk about Marisa. He wasn't, after all, an inarticulate or silent man, and indeed, on many occasions had surprised her by his ability to put into words so vividly what she could only feel.

However, it wasn't until the day that she received the news about the baby that Chloe learned the truth. Later she realised that Marisa must have read the doctor's note, and since she was never exactly placid, the news that Chloe, her hated rival, was to bear Leon's child had driven her into one of her furious rages.

Chloe had been in the beautiful gold and bronze bedroom she shared with Leon when Marisa burst in. The bedroom had been decorated before Leon and Chloe married, and he had given Chloe carte blanche to change the mainly Oriental-inspired decor if she wished, but Chloe hadn't wished. She loved the intricate Chinese lacquer-work; the objets d'art and the beautiful, delicate silk wall panels; richly plumaged birds in bronze and turquoise on a pale gold background; just as she loved the whole ambience of the room.

She had been about to take a shower, having spent

the morning shopping, and had been surprised to see Marisa, who she had understood from the servants was lunching with a friend.

Marisa hadn't beaten about the bush. She came straight to the point, her dark eyes spitting hatred and jealousy as she told Chloe the unpalatable truth: she and Leon were lovers and had been for almost two years.

At first Chloe had simply been unable to believe it, but Marisa had smiled at her, her full lips twisting bitterly, and asked, 'Would I tell you such a shameful thing if it wasn't true? Can you not guess how I feel, knowing that I can never live with him as his wife? That I must always be kept in the background as his "sister"? Why do you think he married a little nobody like you?' Marisa had flung at her. 'Not because he fell in love with your too thin body or your pale blonde hair, whatever he might have told you at the time. No, he married you to protect me! Already I am past the age when most of my contemporaries are married. Soon people will begin to talk. It was to protect me from this talk that Leon married you. A marriage for me, now, is out of the question. No Greek man will take goods despoiled by another, and in the event of someone marrying me, Leon would be called upon by his family to explain how I had come to be despoiled. I cannot see even Leon being able to proffer a satisfactory explanation for that, can you?'

In spite of her fury Chloe had sensed a certain element of satisfaction beneath Marisa's words, but she had been far too distraught to dwell upon it. Leon and Marisa. Leon marrying her simply to protect his half-sister; Leon. . . . No . . .! And yet it all made sense. Horrible, heartbreaking sense, but sense nonetheless. The way he had insisted that they were married almost before she'd had time to catch her breath. His dislike of talking to her about Marisa, and what she had naïvely considered a one-sided and potentially dangerous obsession the younger girl had for her older brother.

Hadn't she herself, in Paris, marvelled and wondered about the fact that someone like Leon should choose her out of all the women who he must have known at one time or another? That was something she hadn't imagined either. She had seen the way in which women looked at him in restaurants; in the streets; and each time a tiny thrill of mingled pleasure and fear had shot through her as she looked up into his darkly male features and wondered what he saw in her.

Now she knew. She had possessed one quality which more than any other had made her a suitable candidate to wear his wedding ring. She was naïve. Add to that the fact that she was desperately in love with him and completely inexperienced and sexually unawaken, and it was no wonder that Leon had urged her into such a precipitate marriage.

And now she was carrying his child!

Marisa must have guessed what was going through her mind, for she pounced, her eyes malicious as she purred acidly:

'Leon won't be pleased. A baby is the last thing he wants—from you! How could he want your child when he knows that he can never re-create himself within the body of the woman he loves?'

'No!'

The despairing protest had been torn from Chloe's throat, but Marisa had ignored her, pressing home her point as she stressed how much Leon loved her and how little he cared about Chloe.

Dimly Chloe remembered stumbling out of the bedroom—no longer a loved retreat where she and Leon could be alone—trying to drag clean, fresh air into lungs suddenly full of cloying nausea.

Marisa followed her, right to the head of the stairs—the apartment was on two floors; bedrooms and staff quarters on the upper storey and reception rooms and kitchen on the lower.

Chloe had hesitated there, trying to clear her brain of the swirling, clogging thoughts, concentrating all her energies on simply trying to stifle the pain which seemed to be a living, breathing entity within her.

Quite how it happened Chloe could not properly remember. One moment she was standing at the top of the stairs, the next she felt Marisa push her sharply and she was falling, screaming out in fright as her body bumped against the stairs.

Her screams had alerted the staff. The housekeeper reached her first. Chloe remembered looking up, her hands clasping her stomach while the older woman looked at her first in horror and then in urgent question, while Marisa hung white-faced on the periphery of her vision, crying and wringing her hands.

Everyone had done all that could be done. In the hospital they were more than kind. Marisa remained at her bedside until Leon got back from Paris—they had insisted on sending for him despite Chloe's protest.

She thought she would never forget how he looked at her when he walked into the ward. She had had to turn her head away so that he wouldn't see the two slow tears rolling down her cheeks. Marisa had gone to him, and they had talked. Then Leon was at her bedside, his expression grim.

'Why?' he had demanded bitterly. 'Why did you destroy my child?'

Chloe knew that the nurses could not understand why, when she had borne so much so bravely, the sight of her husband should cause her to dissolve into tears, but they had had the desired effect. Leon had been bustled discreetly away—not that he showed any desire to linger. No doubt he was anxious to be alone with his mistress, Chloe had thought bitterly, and she had refused to see him the next time he came to the hospital.

On her third day in hospital Leon had insisted on seeing her. He had to return to Paris he told her, but they would talk on his return.

They never did. When she was sure he was safely out of the country, Chloe had discharged herself from hospital and returned to the apartment, where she had taken enough money from her account for her airfare home and her passport, leaving behind her everything but the clothes she stood up in and the plain gold band Leon had placed on her finger the day they were married. Her engagement ring, a huge solitaire diamond, she left on her dressing table with the other jewellery he had given her, and once she returned to England she had removed her wedding ring.

Removing the outward signs of her marriage had been much easier than disposing of the inner ones. It was a year before she could sleep properly at nights, and almost as long before she stopped waking up in the morning with tears on her face.

She replaced the hairbrush and checked that the

bedroom door was firmly closed. There was no way that she could lock Leon out if he did decide to come to her, but she was determined not to be caught off guard; not to allow her body to give in to the persuasive spell which she knew, to her cost, Leon could weave so well.

Leon was an extremely sexually attractive man, she acknowledged, but he was also a liar and a hypocrite. He had never wanted the baby she had lost, but now——now when he was apparently obsessed with the idea of wanting a child, the loss of that child was her fault! She had told him when he came to the hospital what had happened, hoping against hope that Marisa had been wrong, that he did care about her, but he had simply stared at her with cold eyes and compressed lips, his voice metallic with curtness as he said flatly, 'Marisa warned me that you would try to blame her. The guilt is yours, Chloe, and you know it. If you hadn't been so eager to rush out and spend my money you might have been more careful.'

The accusation was so unjust that Chloe had simply gasped, and by the time she had collected her thoughts it was too late. Swept by an emotional storm of grief, she had been incapable of doing anything but begging Leon to go and leave her in peace.

CHAPTER FOUR

CHLOE wasn't sure what had caused her to wake up. Propping herself up on one elbow, she tensed instinctively; searching the darkness of her room, the fine hairs on her bare arms prickling atavistically.

'Leon?'

'You were waiting for me? How flattering. But then you're not a young innocent girl any longer, are you, Chloe? You're a woman, with a woman's desires and needs!'

'Which don't include you!' Chloe flung furiously at him. 'What are you doing in here?'

'At the moment, merely removing my clothes,' came the coolly amused reply, Leon's voice suddenly taking on a biting quality as he added harshly, 'You know full well why I'm here, Chloe, and the sooner. . . .'

'The sooner it's over, the sooner you can have your child and divorce me?' Chloe flung at him, dismayed for some reason to find herself close to tears. Perhaps they had something to do with the fact that a tiny part of her had never stopped grieving for the small life she had lost, and she knew with a sudden blinding flash of insight that there was no way, if Leon succeeded in forcing himself upon her, that she would allow him to take her child from her. Which made it all the more imperative that there should be no child. Biting her lip, she sought desperately for a means of defeating Leon, her concentration constantly disturbed by the small, intimate sounds of clothing being removed, and someone moving about outside the periphery of her vision.

The bathroom door opened and closed; she heard the sound of running water as Leon turned on the shower, and groped hastily for her robe. If she left the bedroom while he was away. . . . Leon's pride was a Greek's pride, as she was fast coming to realise; a man who had felt the lash of his friends' curiosity and pity over a missing wife was hardly likely to pursue that same wife and force her back to her bedroom where any quarrel could be overheard by his staff.

When she reached the security of the drawing room, Chloe snapped on the lights, heaving a sigh of relief. Clear sharp light flooded the room. On a glass coffee table she found a selection of glossy magazines and picked one of them up, flicking through it, sure that even if Leon followed her, he was hardly likely to force a confrontation in so public a place, especially not when he knew that she herself was not going to mask her unwillingness to return to the bedroom with him.

It was not going to be so difficult after all, she reflected when fifteen solitary minutes had passed without a single sound outside the door. All she had to do was to play a waiting game to match Leon's. He no doubt, remembering the past, thought that all he had to do was to make her aware of him and then wait. He was relying on the power of her old adoration of him, but that had gone. As he had so mockingly remarked, she was a woman now, and she would play him at his own game. If she could just keep him at bay until the Kriticos family arrived, surely she could find some means of leaving the island with

them when they left? The excuse of a shopping trip to
Athens, perhaps, something that Leon could not
publicly veto. But he still had her passport. She would
cross that bridge when she came to it, Chloe reflected
tiredly. All at once events were beginning to take
their toll upon her. She settled back on the settee, the
magazine sliding unregarded to her feet, from where
it was removed several minutes later by the tall, dark
male figure who had entered the room and dimmed
the brilliant blaze of lights. He watched the sleeping,
vulnerable figure before him for several seconds, an
unreadable expression on his face, before some sixth
sense penetrated her dreams and Chloe opened her
eyes, Leon's grey ones giving her back her own
shocked reflection.

'Clever Chloe,' he mocked softly. 'But not perhaps
as clever as she thought.'

He had her at a disadvantage, Chloe reflected
bitterly. He seemed to tower above her, the shape of
his body and the male scent of it reaching out to her
as he leaned forward and the brief towelling robe he
was wearing parted to reveal the hard warmth of his
chest.

Chloe swallowed painfully, aware of a sudden con-
striction in her throat. She had forgotten this, either
that or never been wholly aware of it, she thought
weakly, aware of her own quickening pulses and the
sudden uprush of desire which had caught her off
guard; she had forgotten the sensual impact of bare
male flesh; of its subtle arousing scent; its temptation
to fingers which she had already had to clench into
her palms against a wave of longing to reach out and
touch, and go on touching like a blind person seeking
thirstily for knowledge. How could she have forgotten

so much? How could she so easily have dismissed her own vulnerability, the sheer tactile enticement of the body which Leon was knowingly using to break down her defences?

His stance above and around her as he placed a hand either side of her head on the cream silk of the settee was designed, not to intimidate, but to arouse, the light from the lamps he had switched on as he entered the room bathing his lean torso in soft golden light.

'What's the matter?' he mocked, one hand reaching out to gather up the silver softness of her hair and draw it slowly across her throat. The pulse which had started beating there the moment she woke up increased its tempo, a small, frantic, hammering betrayal of his effect upon her senses.

His free hand cupped her jaw, turning her face upward.

'Still my beautiful sea-witch.'

A firm thumb probed the soft curve of her mouth, stroking it sensually.

'Don't!'

Chloe barely recognised her own voice in the husky, despairing croak. Feelings she had not experienced for two years rushed through her as suddenly as though Leon's touch unlocked a secret door. Her body felt curiously weak, heavy, and lethargic with sensations which she recognised as the onset of desire. Panic burst into life inside her and she struggled to sit up, her hands reaching out to push furiously at Leon's chest.

His laughter held mockery and something else—triumph! And as the palms of her hands made contact with the springy dark hairs beneath them, Chloe

knew why. She was powerless to stop her fingers un-
curling against the warmth of skin whose smell and
taste were etched deeply in her senses, and when
Leon's thumb probed the curve of her mouth a second
time her lips parted instinctively, her eyes darkening
with the pain of her body's betrayal as her flesh
tingled beneath his touch.

'Did you honestly think to escape me by coming
here?' Leon murmured against her throat as the silken
softness of her hair was released and his tongue moved
tormentingly against her sensitive flesh. 'How boring
your lovers must be if all they've taught you is that
the place for making love is in the bedroom. . . .'

'Leon, stop it!' His tongue was probing the lobe of
her ear, his teeth nipping her skin into sensual awareness.

Her feeling of lethargy increased. Her body ached
with a tension that had begun somewhere deep inside
her the moment Leon had walked into her room, and
now, with his hands delicately sliding the silk robe
from her shoulders, she was forced to face up to the
truth. No matter how much she might despise Leon—
and herself—oh, how much more herself!—she still
wanted him.

Heat and shame washed over her in alternating
waves, her agonised protest lost, as the thumb which
had been stroking her lips into pliable softness was
suddenly removed and Leon's mouth came down on
her own, obliterating reason and pride. Her lips
parted beneath his in mindless surrender, her small
moan lost beneath the crushing weight of his body as
he joined her on the settee, the hard warmth of his
body against hers turning her lassitude into aching
desire.

'Oh no,' Chloe heard him mutter thickly when she arched instinctively beneath him, 'this isn't something I'm going to hurry—not even for you! I've lived with this moment for two years, and I'm going to enjoy and linger over every second of it, every caress, every kiss. The conception of my son is something you're going to remember for the rest of your life, Chloe, no matter how many men there have been before.'

There was a raw quality to his voice which in another man might have been bitter pain, but in Leon it could only be an indication of how much she had hurt his pride, Chloe acknowledged, her protest dying as he feathered light, tormenting kisses across her face, his hand pushing aside her flimsy robe to find the soft, rounded curve of her breast.

A feeling of faintness overcame her as memories came rushing back. How could she have thought her body capable of resisting Leon, when he had taught it all it knew about sexual response? His lips and tongue were still tormenting her flesh; the slender arch of her throat; the warm curve of her shoulder, her own hands trembling with the effort it cost her to prevent them from sliding against the silken male skin above her.

Marauding male lips had reached the shadowed cleft between her breasts. Chloe stiffened defensively, trying not to look down at the dark head pillowed against her pale flesh. But it was too late; like Pandora she had looked, and her body was punishing her folly by trembling with her growing desire for Leon's complete possession.

She held her breath as his lips played delicately with one firmly erect nipple, heated quivers of pleasure flooding through her. Pleasure she should not be feeling, Chloe reminded herself, gritting her teeth against the small moan of pleasure his touch invoked.

'I know you want me, Chloe,' Leon muttered roughly. 'Your body tells me how much. Like this . . . and this. . . .'

She could only answer him with a ragged sigh of submission; the sigh turning into a gasped sob as his tongue ceased its torment and his mouth closed possessively over the aching flesh it had aroused.

Her fingers clenching automatically in the thick dark hair, Chloe abandoned herself completely to the feverish longing sweeping through her. Nothing mattered except this; this fierce, furious tide of longing sweeping through her, causing her to arch yearningly beneath the taut familiarity of Leon's body, and revel in his unmistakable response.

'Leon. . . .'

At first she thought the female voice was her own, but when Leon stiffened, his hands ceasing their expert arousal of her body, Chloe realised that it was Marisa's.

'Here, put this on,' he muttered, thrusting her robe towards her and also reaching for his own. Furious with herself and bitterly regretting her folly, Chloe fumbled nervously with the sash, but her hands were brushed aside with an impatient oath, as Leon turned her towards him, completing the task just as the door opened to reveal Marisa standing in the door, her voluptuously curved body clearly revealed in the thin robe she was wearing.

'Leon?' Her voice sharpened, her expression darkening as she saw Chloe.

'I was having a nightmare,' she announced, adopting a 'little girl' voice. 'I was frightened. I wanted you, but you weren't in your room. Then I saw lights downstairs. I thought you must be working ...but I didn't realise what was going on,' she added with a spiteful glance at Chloe.

'Marisa!'

Tears formed in her eyes which she made no attempt to wipe away, simply letting them roll down her cheeks, until Leon went across to her, taking her in his arms.

'I was so frightened Leon,' she sobbed, 'and you weren't there. . . . I can't go back to my own room. Can't I stay with you . . .?'

Chloe only just made it to her bathroom in time. The last time she had been so violently sick had been when she was pregnant. Shivering with revulsion, she tore the silk robe from her body and rolled it up into a ball, thrusting it out of sight. Only when she had subjected herself to a long, stinging shower did she return to her bedroom, which was quite, quite empty, but then what had she expected? She was pretty sure that Leon hadn't even been aware that she was there from the moment that Marisa entered the room. Had the other girl only guessed what was happening, or had she known that they were downstairs? Either way, what did it matter?

By rights she ought to be grateful for Marisa's intervention, Chloe reflected, shaken to realise just how close she had come to succumbing to Leon— and not merely succumbing! She had *wanted* him!

Disgusted with herself, she turned on her side, trying to will herself asleep. Whatever else happened she didn't want Leon to know by her pale, wan face

tomorrow morning that she had spent a sleepless
night while he. . . .

While he spent the night with his mistress, she
forced herself to say, appalled by the burning corros-
ively bitter emotion which was her instant reaction to
the words.

Something had happened to her on Eos. Something
had stripped away her normal protective outer skin,
making her ridiculously vulnerable to Leon, and
somehow she had to stop it from happening again. It
galled her to realise just how close she had come to
allowing him to make love to her. It mustn't happen
again—but then tomorrow his guests were arriving
and with a bit of luck she herself would be leaving
with them when their visit came to an end. All she
had to do was to find her passport!

The Kriticos family arrived the following afternoon,
not as Chloe had expected by helicopter, but in a
glittering white yacht which was berthed in Eos's
small harbour.

Chloe had spent the morning carefully avoiding
both Leon and Marisa; the former because she did
not want to have to face the knowledge of her weakness in his eyes and the latter because she was foolishly, searingly jealous of her. Which was ridiculous,
because jealousy was as much a side product of love
as butter was of cream; without one there could not
be the other. But Chloe did not love Leon. She
wanted him, physically, but she despised him—didn't
she? Of course she did, she reassured herself hurriedly.
Her jealousy was merely a legacy of their marriage,
of those early days when she had thought him still a
god in human form come down to earth.

Despite her determination not to make any special effort to make a good impression on Leon's guests, Chloe found herself examining the couture clothes in her wardrobe with a curiosity which soon turned to professional admiration. Surely Leon had not chosen these himself?

From admiring, it was a natural step to trying on a silk two-piece in soft pinks and lilacs, the delicately pleated skirt flattering the long, slender line of her thighs. The bodice was draped softly and seemed to hug the soft curve of her breast. It was an outfit which screamed 'haute couture' to another woman and yet would still draw the admiring glances of men. As it drew Leon's when she entered the salon just in time to see him returning from the small harbour with his guests.

Madame Kriticos was dark and slim, her hair drawn back off her face into an elegant chignon. Make-up, expertly applied, emphasised flashing dark eyes and high cheekbones. Madame Kriticos might be wearing the traditional black of Greek women, but it was Dior black, and Parisienne make-up, and Chloe was glad that she had given in to the traitorous impulse to wear one of her new outfits—doubly glad when the drawing room door was suddenly pushed open and Marisa stormed in wearing skin-tight scarlet jeans and a skimpy tee-shirt which made no secret of the fact that she was not wearing a bra.

Chloe caught Leon's quick, disapproving frown out of the corner of her eye as he drew her forward to introduce Nikos Kriticos. She had already been introduced to his father, a thick-set man of middle height, Greek in physique and outlook, and she turned to his son, preparing the smile that had taken her along so many catwalks and fashion parades.

'*Kiria* Stephanides. . . .' He stammered a little over her name, open admiration in the shy brown eyes looking so uncertainly into hers, and Chloe caught her breath in dismay. Surely Leon could not seriously contemplate a marriage between a boy like this and Marisa, who was centuries older than him in terms of experience?

She suspected that something of her feelings must have shown on her face, because Leon's fingers suddenly tightened warningly on her arm, and she was led away from Nikos to where Madame Kriticos had settled herself on one of the cream silk sofas.

'Yes, Leon, do leave us to talk,' he was instructed by their guest. 'You and Alexandros have much business to discuss, I know. Perhaps Marisa might care to join us. It is a long time since I last spoke to her.' She turned to Chloe, the dark eyes shrewd as she said, 'You have returned to Greece only just in time, I think, Chloe. Marisa is in need of another woman's guiding hand.'

As she spoke her glance drifted across to where Marisa was standing next to Nikos, making no attempt to put the young Greek at his ease, or reply to his stumbling attempts at conversation. 'She dresses like a European girl careless of her virtue,' Madame Kriticos told Leon frankly. 'You do well to find her a husband before it is too late.'

Before Leon could reply, her husband came over to join them, and it was plain from his conversation that Madame Kriticos was correct in saying that the two men had business to discuss.

'Perhaps you will excuse us,' Leon murmured politely, quite obviously to Mr Kriticos' relief. When they had gone Madame Kriticos called over her son and suggested that he ask Marisa to show him the garden.

'It is normally the girl's family who fear to leave her alone in the company of a hot-headed and rash young man, but in this instance, I suspect that Nikos is at considerably more risk than Marisa,' Madame Kriticos informed Chloe when the two younger people had dutifully if somewhat unenthusiastically disappeared into the gardens.

Chloe was still trying to come to terms with her guest's frankness and find some way of responding to her without betraying her own feelings about Marisa when Madame Kriticos, pausing only to invite Chloe to call her 'Christina', added firmly, 'I myself am by no means sure that such a marriage as Leon proposes would be good for Nikos. To my way of thinking he is still too young for marriage, and far too easygoing for a young woman as spoiled and indulged as Marisa, but my husband owes Leon a great deal, and for his sake. . . .' She shrugged. 'Of course there is no denying that in financial terms it would be an excellent match, but there have been rumours circulating Athens for the past six months or more concerning Marisa's behaviour which to put it mildly are—worrying. You have not returned to Greece before time, my dear,' she continued, her eyebrows rising a little as she saw Chloe's expression. She shrugged again, a wholly cosmopolitan gesture. 'Oh, come, Chloe—Leon must have warned you what to expect? Athens society is very enclosed and interbred and delights in gossip, especially when it concerns its brighter stars. Leon is an extremely wealthy man—indeed his wealth causes comment in circles where wealth per se is simply taken for granted. When he returned from Paris with a wife you were the envy of every unmarried Greek girl under twenty-five and every Greek mother over forty. Surely I don't need to tell you of the repercussions for Leon when you left him? Of course everyone expected him to divorce you,' she continued. Chloe daren't react, not with those too shrewd black eyes registering every reflex action she made. 'Especially Marisa,' Christina Kriticos continued. 'I hope I'm not treading on painful corns, my dear, and please don't think I'm speaking only as a mother who resents seeing her only son pushed into marriage with a girl who all too plainly will not make him the kind of wife I have always hoped he might find—but if you intend to make a success of your marriage you must watch out for Marisa.'

When Chloe paled Madame Kriticos smiled thinly. 'Oh, I know Leon thinks she's nothing but a child and is prepared to indulge her every whim, but then men can so seldom see beyond a pretty face, can they? Especially when that face belongs to their nearest relative. Perhaps I shouldn't speak so bluntly,' she continued, allowing Chloe to draw a tiny breath of relief. For one dreadful moment she had thought that Madame Kriticos had known of Leon's real relationship with Marisa. And yet why should that disturb her? Chloe demanded of herself. Surely it was to her advantage for Madame Kriticos to know the truth about Leon, for that would make her own exit from the island all the simpler, and yet her instinctive reaction had been to deny and even lie if necessary to protect Leon. She was still trying to come to grips with this when Madame Kriticos paused, plainly expecting a reply to some question she had posed.

'Oh, I'm so sorry,' Chloe started to apologise. 'I'm afraid my mind. . . .'

'Don't worry about it,' Madame Kriticos laughed, shaking her head. 'I understand from my husband that you and Leon are here on Eos to enjoy a second honeymoon.' Her eyes twinkled. 'Indeed, from what Alexandros told me I think Leon would be grateful if we were to make our visit as short as possible.'

Chloe's smile was constrained. She was remembering what Leon had said about his friends' reaction to their separation. No doubt this was his way of redressing matters. The next step would no doubt be his announcement that his dutiful and docile wife was to produce his son.

'Of course it is a pity that you must have Marisa with you,' Madame Kriticos continued. 'It is a great shame that Leon does not insist on her staying with his Aunt Elena at least until you have had some time together. From what I know of Elena Theopoulos she will not tolerate Marisa's spoiled ways, as Leon does. Those clothes . . .!' Madame Kriticos shuddered and would have said more had the sliding of the patio doors not warned them that Nikos and Marisa were about to enter the room.

Neither of them looked particularly happy. Nikos was flushed beneath his tan, and Marisa looked sulky and bored.

'I'm going to ask Leon to take me to Athens,' she announced, tossing her dark hair, her eyes daring Chloe to comment on her lack of manners. 'I'm bored with Eos.'

Nikos flushed again, and Chloe's hand itched to slap Marisa hard on that part of the anatomy normally reserved for chastising naughty children. Madame Kriticos was quite right. Marisa was a spoiled brat, but beneath the almost typical teenage rebellion and obtuseness was a sly sensuality which jarred on Chloe. No girl of Marisa's age should look out on the world with such cynicism—or such knowledge, and Chloe shivered a little, remembering the look in the dark eyes when Marisa talked of her love for Leon. Marisa she could in some part understand. Her love for Leon was an obsession which she had tended relentlessly, refusing to allow herself to broaden her horizons—in some ways it was to be expected of a girl of such intense emotions, but Leon! Surely he must know what risks he ran in indulging his desire for her? She was his sister! He might be a rich and powerful man, but not rich or powerful enough to place himself beyond the law, or to forfeit the respect of his fellow men.

'Why don't you go and get ready for dinner, Marisa?' Chloe suggested, hoping to avert a further outburst, but to her dismay Marisa turned on her furiously.

'Why? So that you can talk about me behind my back? Say what you like,' she sneered. 'It won't make the slightest bit of difference. If Leon says that Nikos and I are to marry, then marry we will, no matter how much Nikos's mother may object.'

'I'm sorry about that,' Chloe apologised when Marisa had left the room. Madame Kriticos was as still as a statue; Nikos even more embarrassed than he had been before. 'I'm afraid Marisa is going through rather an awkward phase,' she added uncomfortably. 'I think she feels that Leon is being a little high-handed with regard to her marriage, but that was still no reason for her to be so offensive. I shall ask her to apologise, of course. . . .'

'And she will refuse,' Madame Kriticos said dryly. 'I pity you, my dear. If you aren't careful you will have the responsibility of her around your neck like an albatross for the rest of your married life. You must make haste and give Leon a child of his own to cherish.'

And thus displace Marisa from his emotions, Madame Kriticos meant. Little chance of that, Chloe reflected bitterly, but of course she could not tell the other woman the truth.

Voices outside the room proclaimed the return of the men. To Chloe's amazement Leon walked over to her, perching on the arm of the sofa at her side, one arm carelessly but possessively encircling her shoulders and drawing her back against him.

'Where's Marisa?' he asked her.

'Gone to change for dinner.'

Chloe tried to keep her voice as expressionless as possible, but something must have given her away, because Leon's eyes sharpened, his lips hardening as he watched her.

'So, it is very romantic, this reunion of yours,' Alexandros Kriticos commented to Chloe.

'And this time I shall not let her escape,' Leon answered for her, his fingers tightening warningly on her upper arm as he drew her against his body. Chloe could feel his heart beat beneath her cheek. Her proximity didn't affect it in the slightest, while her own pulses were sending erratic warning signals to her brain, and she could feel her flesh weakening with the desire to relax into his warmth and be enveloped by the potent masculinity of his embrace. In an attempt to stem her treacherous thoughts, Chloe forced her muscles to tense in rejection of the pressure of Leon's grasp, and was instantly punished as Leon's head bent, his warm breath fanning her temples, his eyes dark with warning as he added, 'This time I shall give her something to prevent her from wanting to escape. It is amazing how a child tames even the wildest of women.'

'Bravo!' Alexandros cheered. 'Now you are speaking like a true Greek, my friend!'

At last Chloe was free to escape to her room—but it was not her room alone any longer. While she had been entertaining their guests someone—one of the maids, she guessed—had moved Leon's silverbacked brushes and toilet articles into her bathroom. A dark blue silk robe lay carelessly on the bed next to her own nightgown. She tried to breathe and found her throat constricted suddenly with tears.

Tears! What on earth was she crying for? The innocent young girl who had gone too willingly and trustingly into Leon's arms? Hadn't she cried enough tears for her already?

The door opened. She didn't move, her eyes meeting Leon's in the dressing table mirror.

'I won't share this room with you, Leon,' she said with a calm born of desperation. 'And if you try to make me I'll go straight to Madame Kriticos and tell her the truth.'

Without seeming to move Leon was at her side, towering above her as he had done last night, but this time there was no sensuality in the lean body.

Touching her tongue nervously to her lips, Chloe stepped backwards, tensing instinctively against the grip of powerful hands. Only it never came. Instead,

Leon grimaced suddenly, lashes dropping over his eyes to conceal his expression from her, his voice grim as he announced abruptly, 'We're sharing this room, Chloe. I'm not in the mood for argument, especially futile ones, and right now I want to take a shower.' His hand went to his chest to release the buttons of his shirt and Chloe turned quickly away, not wanting to see the lean, muscled lines of his body, not wanting to be reminded of how it had felt to be held close to that body; to be possessed by it, made love to by it. . . .

'Oh no, you don't!'

Leon's harsh voice splintered the silence, spinning her round in shock.

'Don't ever turn away from me in disgust again, Chloe,' he said harshly, reaching out to pinion her wrists. 'Or I warn you I'll give you good reason to feel disgust for me. I'm getting sick and tired of having you look at me as though I'm something that's crawled up out of the gutter. Don't forget, whatever you might claim you feel now, there was a time when you couldn't wait to have me make love to you. . . .'

'No!'

Her protest was instinctive, as much a reaction to his first accusation as his second, but Leon chose to misinterpret it, his face hardening as he dragged her against the hard warmth of his body.

The scent of him filled her nostrils, the feel of him imprinting itself against her yielding flesh. Faintness threatened to overcome her. Chloe put up a hand to fend him off, but it was unnecessary, for Leon had already released her, his expression contemptuous as he walked towards the bathroom, discarding his shirt before pausing by the door.

'You're not just a liar, Chloe,' he told her sardonically, 'you're also a coward. By denying what there was between us you're denying one of life's few real experiences, but it's your life that's made poorer by it, not mine. I'd look the other way, if I were you,' were his parting words as he stepped into the bathroom. 'That is unless you want to be reminded of things you would plainly rather forget—but you haven't forgotten, have you, Chloe!'

More shaken than she cared to admit, Chloe turned her back on him, willing her mind not to play tricks on her by relaying images of Leon as she remembered him, his body as lean and taut as an athlete's, his skin burnished to the colour and texture of bronze. A small moan she wasn't even aware of uttering forced its way past her lips, then her natural courage re-asserted itself.

Leon was trying to intimidate her. Well, two could play at that game! It was true that she hadn't en-visaged having to share a room with him, but it wouldn't be for long! Madame Kriticos plainly did not favour a marriage between Marisa and her son (and after Marisa's behaviour Chloe could scarcely blame her!); she would be anxious to leave, and Chloe was determined to leave with her.

She waited until the sound of the shower had ceased, and then, gathering up clean underclothes, she stalked past Leon, as he thrust open the bathroom door, forcing herself to ignore the silken gleam of water on his skin, the fresh, clean smell of his body, the brief towel knotted over lean hips, crisp dark hairs arrowing downwards over a lean flat stomach. Clenching her hands, Chloe averted her gaze, only giving into the tremors of awareness shuddering through her when she was safely inside the bathroom, behind a locked door.

CHAPTER FIVE

DINNER that night, Chloe found, was something to be endured rather than enjoyed. She might have threatened to expose Leon to the Kriticos', but she knew she was incapable of doing so; her threat had been an idle one, and now she was condemned to sit at the foot of the table watching Marisa flirting openly with Leon, while Madame Kriticos looked on in disapproving silence.

Whether Leon's attention had gone to Marisa's head or whether she was hoping to force the Kriticos family to withdraw from the proposed match Chloe wasn't sure, but there was only one word to describe Marisa's behaviour—provocative!

She was alternately rude and sulky when addressed by anyone apart from Leon. She was wearing a scarlet silk dress which was far too adult, and if Leon were not so obsessed by her Chloe felt sure he must have realised how much she was endangering herself. All her own attempts to smooth over Marisa's open lack of manners were wasted when the girl insisted on continuing to behave badly.

Leon seemed blind to what was going on. He spoke kindly to Nikos, asking him how he enjoyed working with his father, and while Chloe could understand why Leon favoured the match—if he had to lose Marisa to another man then who better than this gentle, self-effacing boy?—she could not help but feel indignant on Nikos' behalf.

After dinner they retired to the drawing room. The evening was warm, and the patio doors were open to allow the breeze to penetrate. Madame Kriticos breathed in the pure air deeply and complimented Leon on the beauty of their surroundings—and its privacy.

'An ideal spot for a honeymoon,' she commented, smiling at Chloe. Marisa's eyes darkened immediately.

'Let's walk in the garden, Leon,' she pleaded, sliding her arm through his and gazing up at him in a manner that made Chloe's heart clench in terror. Surely their guests must see what was happening? It seemed so obvious to her!

'We could go swimming,' she coaxed. 'I love swimming at night . . . the water against my skin, the dark. . . .'

Against her will Chloe's own imagination tormented her with images of Marisa and Leon swimming together, of Leon capturing her and kissing her as he had once kissed Chloe herself, during the balmy days of their honeymoon. She shivered, unaware that Leon was watching her, or of his sudden frown.

'You forget that we have guests, Marisa,' he chided gently. 'Perhaps Nikos would like to walk in the gardens with you.'

He was an excellent actor, Chloe had to give him that. No one watching him could have the slightest inkling of the true relationship between Marisa and himself. Marisa on the other hand was less adroit. At the very mention of walking with Nikos she started to scowl. Chloe held her breath, dreading and yet not knowing how to avert the scene she was sure Marisa was planning.

To her relief Madame Kriticos came to her rescue, albeit unwittingly. 'I should like to walk in the gardens, even if Marisa would not. You shall accompany me, Nikos, since your father cannot as he is expecting a call from Athens.'

'That is so,' Alexandros Kriticos apologised to Leon. 'A business matter which could necessitate our returning to Athens earlier than we had planned.'

Chloe guessed shrewdly that the 'business matter' was merely a product of Madame Kriticos' imagination. No matter what her husband might think she was determined that her son would not marry Marisa, and Chloe could hardly blame her. That meant that she herself would have to move quickly, though. She had to find her passport, and the obvious place to look for it was Leon's study, which was situated in an annexe away from the main bulk of the house. If Leon had not been sharing her room she could have searched the study after everyone else had gone to bed. If she left it until the morning it could well be too late. What on earth was she going to do?

'Are you coming with us, Chloe?' Madame Kriticos asked, rising elegantly to her feet.

'We shall all go—even Alexandros,' Leon announced before she could speak. 'If your call comes through one of the servants will find us. I sometimes think Eos is at its most beautiful at night,' he added. 'Veiled by the darkness, she possesses all the enticement of a woman cloaked in silk. Without the harsh glare of the sun one is not blinded to the allure of the perfumed darkness, so mysteriously enchanting. Darkness imparts its own special magic; one is forced to use other senses than sight; touch, for instance.'

Chloe shivered, half hypnotised by his words into

remembering how it had been to feel his hands touching her body under the protective cover of darkness; how her inhibitions had slipped away and she had felt free to respond to the pagan stirring of her blood. If she and Leon were really lovers, really wanted one another, how onerous the presence of other people on Eos would have been. Both of them would have been longing for them to leave so that they could wander through the darkness alone, stopping occasionally to kiss and touch, and perhaps even make love in a shadowed grove with only the stars to witness their wordless communion with each other and their universe.

'Chloe, are you all right?'

The sharp enquiry jerked her back to her surroundings. Everyone else was standing by the door, and suddenly she realised that here was her excuse to search Leon's study undetected.

'It's just a headache,' she lied. 'I'll be all right, but if you don't mind I think I'll go and lie down. . . .'

'Oh, but you should come,' Madame Kriticos protested. 'The fresh air will do you good. Tell her, Leon. . . .'

'Oh, come on, Leon, or are we going to wait all night? She's probably making it up about the headache anyway,' Marisa burst out scornfully. 'Isn't that what Englishwomen always say when they don't want to make love?'

There was a tiny silence and then Madame Kriticos was saying lightly, 'Really, Leon, that child definitely needs taking in hand,' and Chloe was free to make her escape while Leon ushered Marisa and his guests out on to the patio.

What was Marisa trying to do? Persuade Leon to

change his mind? Didn't she already have enough, Chloe asked herself bitterly, or was it that she couldn't bear to think of anyone bearing Leon a child if she couldn't do so herself? Well, Marisa needn't worry. If she could find her passport the moment the Kriticoses showed any sign of leaving, she was going with them, Chloe decided bitterly.

She waited ten minutes before walking quickly out of the drawing room and down to the study.

She hadn't been inside the room before, and at first was startled by the starkness revealed to her by the bright moonlight. Unwilling to risk putting on the light, she was grateful for the full moon which shone brightly into the room. The walls were plain and white, offset by a richly polished floor ornamented by a brilliantly coloured Oriental rug. A large desk dominated the room, one entire wall covered in bookshelves and custom-built cupboards which Chloe guessed must be filing cabinets, although they looked more like expensive pieces of furniture.

Where to start, that was the problem. Funnily enough, now that she was in the study, and even though she knew she had the right to regain her property, she felt a stupid reluctance to start going through Leon's private documents.

Telling herself that she was being foolish, she forced herself to overcome this aversion, slowly opening the first of the right-hand set of desk drawers. It was immaculately tidy, files and papers sorted neatly away. Chloe flicked through them, telling herself that she had no reason to feel so guilty, so grubby.

The second drawer revealed merely a diary and an address book. How much longer did she have before everyone returned? Chloe wondered anxiously. Her heart was thumping nervously, she could feel her skin grow damp with perspiration as she closed the second drawer and moved feverishly to the other side of the desk. It was locked! She tugged the handle disbelievingly, disappointment overcoming caution as she stamped her foot and muttered under her breath, 'I might have known!'

'Indeed you might—just as *I* might have known that your indisposition was merely a fabrication. Just as, in fact, I did know that it was a fabrication,' Leon said sardonically, arms across his chest as he lounged in the doorway. 'Is this what you were looking for?' With one lithe stride he crossed the room, unlocking the desk drawer with a key which he produced from his pocket, withdrawing the familiar dark blue of Chloe's passport.

'Give it to me . . . please,' she begged, her voice suddenly constricted. For a moment when she had looked up and seen him framed in the doorway she had been overcome by a feeling as pagan as the gods themselves.

'Only when you have given me my son,' Leon drawled softly, cutting across her thoughts. 'A fair exchange, is it not? Your freedom for my child. . . .'

'Our child, don't you mean?' Chloe burst out furiously. 'You can't make me do this, Leon! It isn't . . . it isn't human! How can you expect me to carry your child for nine months and then calmly hand it over to you and disappear out of its life for ever? Even women who are paid to do that have second thoughts. Mother-love is such an overwhelmingly strong emotion,' she murmured, more to herself than the man watching her. 'I don't think. . . .'

'What? That your freedom is payment enough?'

Leon goaded. 'What else had you in mind? Money? Jewels?'

'Why, you. . . .'

The marks left on the lean tanned cheek shocked Chloe more than the recipient of her instinctive reaction. The echoe of her dismayed breath seemed to reverberate around the enclosed silence of the room, making her suddenly aware of the fact that Leon must have returned alone from his walk.

'Satisfied? Does that expression of your assumed outrage make you feel better?'

'Only one thing will make me feel better,' Chloe said bitterly, 'and that's being free of you, and this island.'

'And so you will be,' Leon said evenly, 'just as soon as you give me my son.'

'Never!'

The gauntlet was thrown beyond recall, and Chloe stood as stiff as a ramrod, her hair a silver curtain round her slender shoulders, her eyes wide with nervous apprehension.

Another man might have been moved to pity by her obvious dread, but Leon merely smiled cynically, one hand reaching up towards her throat, his fingers sliding through the silken net of her hair, the dark eyes mesmerising her into stillness as his fingers threaded through her hair to the base of her skull, where their firm pressure forced her head up and back, his dark head blotting out the moonlight as his mouth took hers in a kiss that possessed ruthlessly, barely concealing an anger which seemed to reach out to a deeply hidden core within Chloe, releasing her own bitterness in a storm of emotion which left her fighting the possession of his mouth as furiously as he reinforced it.

At last, as though growing tired of her rebellion, Leon punished her defiance with lips that seared and branded, the steel grip of his fingers completely preventing her from moving, as he eased her tightly clamped lips apart and enforced upon her a kiss which admitted no hindrance.

The hand which was not constraining her head swept downward, pushing aside the flimsy fabric of her dress, cupping her breast and ruthlessly punishing the tender flesh, until the last of Chloe's slender self-control snapped and his touch sent her shuddering into his arms, lost to everything but the dark tide of emotion surging up inside her.

'You want me, Chloe, don't try to deny it,' she heard Leon mutter thickly from a distance. 'Stop making it harder for yourself. There's nothing to be ashamed of in feeling desire, and you do feel desire,' he groaned against her skin. 'We both do. . . .'

That restored Chloe to sanity. She took advantage of his relaxed grip to push him away, running shaking fingers through her tangled hair.

'I'm not a romantic teenager any more, Leon,' she reminded him brittlely. 'Those sort of facile arguments might have worked once, but not now. Desire might be enough for you, but it isn't for me!'

She would have left him, but he reached for her suddenly, frowning as he stared out into the garden.

'The others are back,' he said briefly. 'Marisa doesn't seem to be getting on very well with Nikos.'

'Are you surprised?' Chloe demanded. 'Madame Kriticos is, quite naturally, concerned about the match.'

'And you, of course, did nothing to persuade her

otherwise?' Leon commented, his lips twisting a little. 'How your sex delights in inflicting wounds upon itself! I know you and Marisa have had your differences in the past, but. . . .'

'It's got nothing to do with how I feel about Marisa,' Chloe burst out impetuously. 'Leon, how can you contemplate such a marriage when all the time . . . all the time. . . .' Strange how even now she found it difficult to put his relationship with his half-sister into words. 'You know what I mean,' she finished lamely. 'I feel so sorry for poor Nikos.'

'So, there you are!' Madame Kriticos' voice rang out gaily. 'You should have come with us, Chloe,' she continued. 'Leon had no taste for the moonlight without you.'

Chloe forced herself to join in the general laughter, absurdly conscious of Leon's hand on the back of her neck, of the strong, dark hairs curling with arrogant maleness against the crisp white cuff of his shirt. A lump rose in her throat, her eyes aching with unshed tears.

'If you'll all excuse me, I think I'll go to bed,' she murmured, wriggling free of Leon's grip. In the passage she bumped into Marisa, who favoured her with a bitter, burning glare.

It was a relief to reach her bedroom—no, not 'her' bedroom any more, Chloe thought half hysterically, for from tonight she would be sharing her room—and her bed—with Leon.

She couldn't bring herself to prepare for bed, or to do anything that would give Leon the opportunity to claim that she might welcome his advances, and even though her body craved sleep, her mind kept her awake.

It was two o'clock before she heard his footsteps outside the door; he walked into the room without seeing her, tugging impatiently at his dinner jacket, which he flung carelessly on to the bed, pausing only when he realised that she was not in it, but sitting in a chair.

'For Pete's sake Chloe!' he protested wearily when he did see her. 'No more arguments—not tonight. Alexandros has just informed me that his wife does not think that Marisa will make Nikos a good wife. It was an extremely embarrassing interview—for both of us.'

In spite of herself, Chloe felt a small tug of sympathy. To hide it she said coolly,

'It's probably just as well. Even if the Kriticoses had been willing you would never have managed to persuade Marisa to go through with it.'

'Marisa is a child, and still under my guardianship,' Leon replied briefly, frowning. 'She will do as she is told.'

'Even if it means marrying someone she doesn't love?' Chloe retorted mildly.

'Something which you know all about, of course,' Leon mocked cynically, pushing his broad shoulders off the wall where he had been leaning. 'Haven't you learned yet, my lovely wife, that we can never pass on to others the benefit of our own bitter experience?'

'You're drunk,' she accused, suddenly catching the smell of spirits on his breath.

'I've been drinking,' he corrected, wrenching open the thin silk shirt he had been wearing beneath his dinner jacket. 'But I am not drunk—there is a difference. Oh, don't bother to look at me like that— as though you were suddenly looking upon the face of the devil!' Leon swore angrily. 'I'm a man like any other, Chloe, with the same needs and desires. I like the feel of the sun's heat on my body, the silken caress of the sea; I like to eat, drink, and make love. I want to hold my child. . . .'

How close he had come to slipping under her guard, Chloe thought breathlessly. All at once the room seemed to be stifling her, the walls closing in on her.

'I'm . . . I'm going out for a walk,' she said shakily. 'I want a breath of fresh air. I. . . .'

She was completely unprepared for the savagery with which Leon took hold of her, fury smouldering deep within the grey eyes, the hard bones of his face tensed beneath the brown silk of his skin.

'What are you trying to tell me?' he demanded thickly. 'That you can no longer bear even to breathe the same air, because it is so contaminated? Enough! You are my wife, Chloe, and you will bear my child. I would be within my rights to enforce my possession of you—well within them, according to Greek law!'

'Then what's stopping you?' Chloe flung back, forgetting all her good intentions of not arousing him to anger. 'Why stop at physically possessing me against my will when you've practically kidnapped me and forced me to live here with you, or does your pride stick at the thought of having to force a woman to accept your embraces? Is that it, Leon? Do you want the sop to your vanity of believing that I might come to you willingly?'

'You did before—more than willingly,' Leon reminded her huskily. 'It could be like that between us again, Chloe.'

His fingers reached out and touched her arm, the

tiny hairs lifting beneath the brief caress.

'Don't touch me!' The angry words were as much a product of her own melting reaction as Leon's cool familiarity, but he was not to know it, and watching his eyes darken to the colour of slate, Chloe wished the words unsaid, fear shivering along her spine as Leon bit out grittily,

'You little hypocrite! You wanted me once before, I can make you want me again.'

'Physically perhaps,' Chloe agreed coolly, inwardly marvelling at her own apparent calmness. 'But there's more to a relationship between two people than physical arousal. Leon, what are you doing?' she asked curiously, as he re-buttoned his shirt.

'Now it's my turn to feel the need for fresh air,' he mocked. 'I've had a surfeit of maudlin sentiment, I find it . . . cloying. Don't bother to wait up for me.'

Where had he gone? Chloe wondered as the door closed behind him. To Marisa?

Wherever it was, he only returned in the early hours of the morning to leave again before the sun streaming in through the windows awoke Chloe to an empty bed, only the dented pillow at her side proof that she had not slept alone. A weakening sensation she was glad Leon was not there to witness stole through her as she remembered other mornings when she had awoken to find him beside her. A sigh trembled past her lips, followed by an intense sensation of loss. Pushing the feeling aside, Chloe showered and dressed.

Breakfast was being served on the patio, Gina told her, and Chloe was just drinking her second cup of coffee when the Kriticos family arrived.

'I don't know whether it is the sea air, or the lack

of traffic, but I slept far longer than I normally do,'
Madame Kriticos laughed. 'How lucky you are to
live on this beautiful island, my dear.'

'How lucky she is to have a husband wealthy
enough to be able to afford such luxuries,' Alexandros
joked.

It had apparently been agreed that they would
remain on Eos for another day—a sop to convention
and good manners, Chloe suspected. There had been
no sign of Marisa at the breakfast table and Nikos
had brightened considerably when he realised that
she was not there. Somehow, between now and when
the Kriticoses left, she had to get her passport and get
on board their yacht without Leon becoming aware
of what she was doing.

After breakfast, Nikos asked rather shyly if she
knew where the island's best beaches were situated.
It transpired that he preferred to bathe in the sea
rather than use the pool, and as Madame Kriticos
was not feeling very energetic, and her husband had
business to discuss with Leon, Chloe offered to go
with Nikos to the beach.

The housekeeper, Katina, gave them instructions
how they might find a small, secluded sandy cove on
the more sheltered side of the island, and they set off
shortly after breakfast in Leon's rugged jeep, a
hamper of food in the back.

'You will not forget that we are leaving later this
afternoon, will you, Nikos?' Madame Kriticos
reminded her son as they left. Chloe hadn't seen anything of Leon since getting up, nor of Marisa, and she
wondered if Leon had told the other girl that she
wasn't to be forced into marriage after all.

The cove was at the far end of the island, sheltered

by rugged cliffs, and in order to reach it they had to park the jeep at the top and walk down a narrow flight of steps cut into the rock. Nikos went first, pausing frequently to make sure that Chloe was all right. As he had the hamper in one hand and their towels in another, Chloe found his concern rather touching.

'I am not quite so old and decrepit that I can't manage a few steps,' she teased him at one point. Nikos had already reached the cove and was turning to assist her down the last few steps, his brown eyes warm with unhidden admiration as they studied her curves, covered only by brief shorts and a halter-necked top.

'Not old at all,' he breathed fervently. 'You are very beautiful, Madame . . . very beautiful,' he added softly, gazing at her hair. 'Leon is a very lucky man.'

'Stop flattering me,' Chloe commanded. 'We came here to swim, remember!'

She was already wearing her bikini beneath her shorts and top and felt no inhibitions about removing them in Nikos' company. The sea felt like silk against her heated skin, and she revelled in its gentle buoyancy, calling to Nikos as he raced down the beach to join her, a lithe figure in close-fitting white briefs. 'You were right—this is much, much better than the pool.'

She floated on her back while Nikos performed an energetic crawl out to a rock in the middle of the small bay, closing her eyes and letting the waves lap her into a semi-somnolent state.

A sudden spray of sea water on her face roused her. Nikos was treading water at her side, grinning mischievously.

'It's lunchtime,' Chloe informed him. 'Race you to the beach!'

Even with the head start he gave her she had trouble keeping up with him. He was a powerful swimmer—just as Leon was. Leon! It was as though a cloud passed over the sun, the very thought of her husband's name reminding her of her plight.

Over lunch she questioned Nikos discreetly about the yacht, hoping to discover the best place to conceal herself until they were safely out to sea.

There were half a dozen main cabins, he told her; four aft and two forward. The forward cabins were the most luxurious, he explained, but at present they were being refurbished, so they weren't in use.

While they talked Chloe's thoughts were busy. If she could just get her passport, and find a way to smuggle herself on board the yacht—she had abandoned the idea of pleading the excuse of a shopping trip, because she felt sure that Leon would find some means of preventing her from leaving—she was sure she could conceal herself in the unused cabin, she hoped, until they reached Athens, but she was still reluctant to involve anyone else in her affairs or to confide in anyone, however sympathetic, the truth concerning Leon's reasons for taking her to Eos.

After lunch Chloe sunbathed for a while, while Nikos explored the beach. Later they swam together, drying off in the sun before preparing to return to the villa. Nikos was a pleasant companion, Chloe reflected, when the latter suggested that she might want the beach to herself for changing her clothes.

'My bikini is dry now,' she assured him, standing up to brush sand off it. 'I'll just put my shorts and top on over it. After all, we haven't got far to go.' As she spoke, she stepped backwards on to the sharp, exposed edge of a shell, pain momentarily robbing her of balance. She put her hand out towards Nikos instinctively, grateful for the warm grip of his fingers as he grasped her arm, neither of them aware, as he knelt at her feet to examine the wound, of the tall, tautly male figure watching them from above.

'Thank goodness it hasn't punctured the skin!' Chloe exclaimed, tentatively replacing her foot on the sand and disengaging herself. 'I ought to have been more careful.'

Assuring Nikos that she was perfectly all right, she followed him up the steps to the jeep.

There was no one on the patio when they reached the villa. Everyone else had gathered in the salon for drinks, Maria explained to Chloe as she stepped into the hall.

Chloe was under the shower when she heard the door open. She reached instinctively for the towel, freezing as she saw Leon approaching her, his face a mask of controlled rage.

'What are you trying to do?' he grated furiously. 'Wash away the caress of your lover? I saw you,' he added before Chloe could protest. 'So don't waste your time lying to me. No wonder you didn't want Marisa to marry him!'

'Leon, you. . . .' She gasped as her towel slipped, and bent to retrieve it, colour stinging her cheeks as Leon's glance slid slowly along the length of her body, taking in the firm, high thrust of her breasts and the softly rounded swell of her stomach before he said curtly,

'Think yourself fortunate that my duties to my guests prevent me from punishing you as a Greek does punish his wife for behaviour such as yours. And remember, tonight our guests leave and you and I will be alone.'

He said it with such a wealth of grim satisfaction that it was several seconds after he had left the room before Chloe could bring herself to start dressing.

She was just applying a touch of frosted eyeshadow when Marisa walked in without bothering to knock.

'I wanted Leon,' she announced with cool insolence, staring round the room. 'Where is he?'

'Not here,' Chloe replied equally coolly, refusing to be rattled by the other girl's objectionable behaviour.

'How can you stay?' Marisa hissed suddenly, 'knowing that he doesn't really want you. That all he wants is the child he can give you.'

'How can I not?' Chloe retorted, putting down the eyeshadow, and turning to face her. 'There's the small matter of my passport, for one thing, and for another. . . .'

She wasn't allowed to get any farther.

'You mean if you had your passport you'd leave?' Marisa demanded eagerly. 'But how?'

'I'd find a way.' Chloe felt too suspicious of Marisa to trust her with the truth, despite the fact that she knew the other girl longed for her to leave. She didn't trust her perverted thinking not to lead her into going straight to Leon and telling him what Chloe had in mind.

'You'd really go?'

'Like a shot,' Chloe replied dryly, frowning when Marisa walked to the door purposefully. 'What are you doing?'

'I'm going to get your passport. It will be locked in

Leon's desk and I know where he keeps the spare key. If I give it to you will you promise to leave and never come back?' she demanded fiercely.

Chloe nodded her head. Poor Marisa, in so many ways she was such a child still, a child whose adolescence had been tragically marred by her relationship with Leon, so mature and yet at times so very childish.

'I'll give you the passport after dinner,' Marisa promised. 'I'll meet you by the pool.'

During dinner she was so different from the sulky creature of the previous evening that Chloe was not surprised to see Leon watching her. What was he thinking, she wondered, this man ruthless enough to force the girl who loved him, and whom he loved, into an unwanted marriage, simply so that he could have a child with the wife he had married purely to conceal his incestuous affair?

'You must visit us in Athens,' Madame Kriticos was saying to Chloe. 'We shall go shopping together. You must arrange it, Leon. Bring her with you the next time you come to Athens on business.'

'I shall not be visiting Athens again for another three months,' Leon responded, 'by which time my wife might not be feeling like air or sea travel. . . .'

Marisa frowned. 'But we always go to Athens in the autumn.'

'Then this year must be the exception,' Leon said quietly. 'Although of course if you wish to go, Marisa, I can make arrangements for you to stay with friends.'

Had he no pity or compassion? Chloe wondered, looking at Marisa's pale face. Surely he could see what effect his words had upon her?

Madame Kriticos had obviously witnessed Marisa's distress, because when she and Chloe were alone, she confided warningly, 'My dear, it is none of my business, but Marisa is far too emotionally involved with Leon. If you want my advice, a few months in Athens under the eye of some stern matron is exactly what she needs.'

The Kriticos family were leaving at ten o'clock, and they had dined early to make sure that they were not delayed. Chloe was to meet Marisa by the pool at nine, and when she slipped outside into the velvet darkness of the night, at first she thought that Marisa was not going to come. She had been waiting ten minutes and was on the point of giving up when the Greek girl suddenly materialised at her side, grasping a familiar slender dark blue rectangle.

'Here you are,' she announced, pushing it towards Chloe. 'I've fulfilled my part of the bargain—now it's up to you to fulfil yours. If you don't I'll make you sorry you were ever born! It's me Leon loves. Me, do you understand?'

She was gone before Chloe could reply, vanishing into the darkness like a wraith.

Slowly Chloe looked down. Yes, it was her passport. She drew a trembling sigh. All she had to do now was to get down to the yacht and conceal herself there without anyone being aware of her absence. A Herculean task, but no more so than the one already accomplished!

CHAPTER SIX

In the end it was amazingly easy.

They were not to go down to the yacht with them, Madame Kriticos insisted. There was a cool breeze, and anyway, she hated goodbyes, and so, while Leon drove them down to the boat with their luggage, Chloe slipped out into the night, using the short cut which avoided the island's one road, and reached the harbour well before there was any sign of the car.

There was no one guarding the gangplank—why should there be? And although there were signs of activity on board, no one seemed to notice Chloe as she slipped from the shadows and up on deck.

It wasn't easy, feeling her way around in the dark. The companionway was steep and the corridor at the bottom of it inky black. Chloe was just starting to feel her way gingerly along the wall when sounds from above panicked her into opening the first door she came to and darting inside.

The cabin was in complete darkness, even the portholes apparently covered, and it was impossible for her to see anything of her surroundings. Beneath her feet she could feel the steady thrum of the powerful engines. Seconds, or was it a lifetime, seemed to drag past, fear grasping her by the throat as she waited, listening for the sounds of footsteps approaching. No one came. Perhaps the Kriticoses wouldn't come down until after they had sailed.

Now, with time to think clearly, Chloe acknowledged the extent of her previous danger—as much from herself as Leon. With frighteningly little effort she could recall every smallest detail about him—the involuntary flexing of his muscles as he walked, the look in his eyes when he was aroused, the feelings his presence brought to life within her. Feelings which had brought her close to the brink of giving in to him on more than one occasion!

The engine note changed; the yacht surged forward, out into the purple Aegean night, the silence so intense that Chloe could hear the swift slap of water along the bows. In her mind's eye she pictured the white vessel cleaving the dark water, graceful as a bird, and a shuddering sigh broke from her lips.

Groping her way round the cabin, she came to a bed and sank weakly down on to the edge of it. She had done it! She had escaped from Eos, from Leon. So why should she feel this nagging sense of anti-climax, of disappointment almost?

The cabin door swung inwards suddenly, the light dazzling eyes now accustomed to almost Stygian darkness, and Chloe gathered her defences, clearing her throat as she prepared her speech of apology and explanation. A quarrel was how she had decided to explain her flight from Leon, and she was so busy rehearing the words that she was almost upon the tall figure standing in the illuminated doorway before she realised who it was, his name whispering past lips suddenly stiff with shock.

'Leon!'

'Surprised?'

He stepped forward into the cabin, closing the door behind him and reaching for a light switch. A subdued mushroom glow illuminted a cabin far more luxuriously appointed than any bedroom Chloe had ever seen in her life, and despite her shock she was still awed enough to register peach silk curtains matching the beautiful embroidered bedspread and stylish fitted furniture of a type she had only ever glimpsed enviously in prestige glossy magazines. A deep-pile peach carpet covered the floor, and adjacent to the door to the corridor was another one which she guessed must lead to an en-suite bathroom.

'The master stateroom,' Leon drawled, breaking the silence. 'Like it?'

'What are *you* doing here?' Chloe demanded, ignoring his question. He was the last person she had wanted to see, and her eyes clung despairingly to the closed door, willing either her unwitting host or hostess to appear and rescue her.

'I could ask that question of you,' Leon retorted. 'But it would be a pointless exercise, since we both know exactly what you're doing here, or what you think you're doing here. You were trying to escape from me, weren't you? Trying to use the Kriticoses' departure as a means of leaving Eos yourself.'

'And I've succeeded,' Chloe replied bravely, her eyes measuring the distance between herself and the door. Surely Leon didn't mean to provoke a scene in front of his friends?

'Have you?'

The softly spoken words were like a splash of ice cold water.

'Of course I have!' Chloe cried. 'And if you don't let me disembark at Athens I'll tell your friends everything. . . .'

'Everything?' The word was drawled softly, but

beneath Chloe sensed bitter anger. 'Like how you forced the lock on my desk, after trying to persuade Marisa to do it for you, and then removed your passport? Will you tell them that, Chloe? Or,' he added softly before she could correct him, before she could take in what he had said properly, 'should I say that is what you would tell them, were they here to be told?' He smiled suddenly, the brief gesture devoid of any humour or genuine amusement, and so cold that it struck terror into Chloe's heart. 'You see, my dear wife, you were clever, but not clever enough. Alexandros had left some papers in my study before dinner and when I went to retrieve them for him I discovered the forced lock on my desk. As if that wasn't enough to incriminate you,' he added acidly, 'Marisa came to me just before I came down here to confess that you had asked her to search my desk, thinking quite rightly that I would be less suspicious of her than I would of you. The moment I realised that you had retrieved your passport I guessed what you would do. My own yacht, the *Nemesis*, was at anchor in the bay on the other side of the harbour—I had ordered it moved there when our guests arrived, and it was a simple matter to switch vessels.'

'Your yacht . . .' Chloe stared disbelievingly up at him. 'You mean that . . . I. . . .'

'You, my dear Chloe, might have escaped from Eos,' he agreed smoothly, 'but you have merely exchanged one prison for another. The *Nemesis* belongs to me and you and I are the only passengers on it. A fittingly romantic venue, wouldn't you think, in which to conduct our . . . affairs.'

'Let me go!'

Chloe flew past him, wrenching open the door, but

she didn't get very far before her flight was impeded by the strong male arms reaching out to grasp and almost swing her off her feet.

'To where?' Leon mocked, his lips twisting in bitterness. 'Or were you intending to throw yourself overboard in true theatrical style?'

'Even that would be better than being forced to endure you!' Chloe flung at him, close to hysteria. 'I'm not staying here with you. I. . . .'

'Enough!'

The crisp word silenced her protests, the sudden economy of movement which carried her across the peach carpet to be deposited none too gently on the bed warned her that Leon's patience was coming to an end.

'I am asking no more from you than is my right—than you owe me,' she was told in curt tones. 'Had you not been so foolish before, none of this would have been necessary.'

'By "foolish" I suppose you mean if Marisa hadn't pushed me . . . Oh, I'm sorry,' she apologised insincerely. 'If I hadn't "fallen" and lost the baby, I'd be free of you now. How can you be so callous—so coldblooded?' she demanded. 'Have you any idea what it feels like to be treated as a . . . brood mare?'

'None,' was the uncompromising response. 'But I do have some experience of how it feels to be treated as a free meal-ticket; to be married purely for financial gain and then have my wife run out on me when she's had enough. Why didn't you divorce me? Or can I guess?' he asked bitterly. 'The longer the marriage exists, even if only on paper, the higher the eventual settlement, isn't that how it goes?'

Tears shimmered in Chloe's eyes, and she turned

away. Why hadn't she divorced him? Deep in her heart she knew why. Because foolishly she had never stopped loving him; never stopped hoping that one day. . . .

'Are you trying to say that I married you for your money?' she demanded at last when she had control of her vocal chords.

'Are you trying to say that you didn't?' Leon asked with a cynical twist of his lips. 'Let's not play games with one another, Chloe, and let's get one thing understood. I always insist on getting value for money. So far you've proved to be a less than good investment, and I've decided to do what any businessman of sense does in such circumstances.'

'You mean divorce me?' Chloe asked, dry-eyed. What a time to discover that she still loved him! The situation had definite overtones of black comedy!

'Later,' Leon agreed coolly. 'But firstly I intend to realise my assets, get what benefit I can from my investment before I dispose of it. Think of it as buying yourself a comfortable old age,' he goaded softly. 'Or if that won't do, think of whatever you thought of when we were first married, and you managed to receive my . . . embraces with such a touching display of pseudo-enthusiasm. Take care, Chloe,' he told her harshly, grasping the small fist she had instinctively raised. 'I could make it harder for you. . . .'

'I won't do it,' Chloe announced positively.

'You don't have any say in the matter.' The soft reminder jerked her into real awareness of her situation. To all intents and purposes she was alone on the yacht with Leon—for she knew that none of his men would so much as lift a finger to help her, if she went to them, and she could tell by the harsh set of his mouth that he was way, way beyond the stage of pandering to her wishes.

'No protests? But then you can't morally raise any really, can you? Let's be honest with each other for once. I'll make it easy for you. Marisa has told me what you said to her. . . .'

Chloe stared at him, waiting. Marisa had been very busy, she thought bitterly. First she had told Leon that she had tried to persuade her to break into his desk, and now. . . . What exactly had she told him?

She soon learned.

'You told her that you had only married me because of my wealth, didn't you?' he demanded without emotion. 'You told her that having my child had never been part of your plans, and never would be. Well, you know what they say about "plans", don't you?'

All at once his voice was soft with a menace that made the tiny hairs on Chloe's body stand up in terror. She wanted to deny that she had ever said any such things, but her tongue seemed to have cleaved to the roof of her mouth and she could only stand and stare like a small frozen statue as Leon advanced upon her.

'Well, if we're going to reduce our relationship to terms of who owns what, I seem to remember that I was the one to provide you with this dress.' He grasped the soft pale green silk as he spoke and Chloe could only watch in growing sickness as his grip tightened and he said slowly, 'Which according to your rules give me the right to do whatever I choose with it—which is this.'

Chloe gasped once as she felt the frail silk tear and

then closed her eyes, unable to bear the look of near-hatred in Leon's as he looked down at the slender shape of her body.

'I don't know what I hate you for the most, Chloe,' he muttered thickly as he scooped up her stiff body and lowered it on to the bed, 'killing my child or destroying my faith in my own judgment. I thought you a shy innocent child, when in reality. . . . I should have known, I suppose. Living as you did in the world of high fashion you were still a virgin, and I should have guessed then that it was not innocence but shrewdness; a knowledge of how much such a gift would mean to the man with enough money to pay for it. A man like me.'

'No!'

The word was dragged out of her in a long moan, her face as pale as milk against the peach silk. She felt as though someone were cutting out her heart with burning knives; even the pain she had felt on learning that Leon loved his half-sister had not compared with this raw, scorching agony she knew now.

'Yes!' Leon bent towards her, his face suffused with dull bitter colour beneath his tan, his eyes burning in his set face. 'Yes, yes, yes. Say it, Chloe. Admit it!'

She turned away, but his fingers grasped her jaw, forcing it round. 'Say it,' he demanded hoarsely, 'I want to hear you admit it with my own ears.'

'It isn't true!' To her horror Chloe felt tears form and well in her eyes, burning like acid as they slid down pale cheeks and on to the lean brown fingers, cupping her face in a parody of the tenderness of a lover.

'You're a liar, Chloe! Didn't your mother warn

you that you would be punished for telling lies?'

He was punishing her; his lips feathering light, tormenting kisses against the vulnerable curve of her throat, his hands caressing her skin.

'I'm not lying!'

Her defiance brought swift retaliation.

'Oh, come on! There's no need to keep up the pretence now.' The lips which had been tormenting her skin curved downwards in cynical disbelief. 'We both know the truth—now! What a pity I wasn't aware of it beforehand, I could have made sure that I got my money's worth. However, it isn't too late. I still have tonight to remedy matters.'

'Leon. . . .'

'Don't waste your time pleading with me,' she was told harshly. 'There's a word for people who take money under false pretences. They're called cheats, and I don't like being cheated, Chloe.'

She was frightened then for the first time, sensing the anger banked down inside him, feeling it in the bitter pressure of his mouth as it closed on hers, his hands pinioning her wrists to the pillows behind her. She tried to escape, to free her mouth from the hot, grinding pressure of his, but he was far too strong for her, and for all his obvious contempt and rage, to her dismay she could feel the desire beating up inside him, and knew that for some reason his fury had acted like some powerful aphrodisiac, from whose effect she wasn't entirely free herself.

It was degrading, she told herself, curling her fingers into small tense fists; trying not to succumb to the force he was using to part the lips she had closed against him in silent defiance, and yet in spite of logic and common sense some part of her thrilled to the dominance of his touch, her body responding as though to some deeply ingrained programming, which made it impossible for her to reject him entirely. The warm aroused scent of his body filled her nostrils, the heavy pressure of his body, forcing her own back into the bed, making her aware of his growing desire. One wrist was released as he sought for and found the fastening of her brief lacy bra, his hand cupping the soft fullness far more effectively than the small scrap of satin had ever done. His fingers stroked and teased, knowing just how to evoke the response he wanted. Groaning her dismay, Chloe gasped when the involuntary parting of her lips was ruthlessly utilised to enforce a kiss that brutalised and ravaged the soft inner flesh of her mouth until she could taste blood.

'Leon!'

Her protest was as much against herself as him—a fear that she could all too easily be sucked down by the powerful undertow of a passion which threatened to overcome her like black velvet darkness. She tried to tell herself that passion on its own was degrading, meaningless, and insulting, but the emotions she had dammed up for so long broke through the barriers of her principles, and it was fatally easy to forget why Leon was making love to her and remember only the golden days of their honeymoon.

'Leon. . . .' The word was stifled beneath the mouth imposing its dominance on hers, and as another wave of desire made her tremble beneath it, Chloe acknowledged the fear that had been at the back of her mind since Leon had come back into her life—she still loved him!

Once acknowledged, the truth was like a catalyst

deep down inside her, all the traitorous impulses she had so valiantly controlled turning on her in outright rebellion, her small, heated moans of protest as Leon's mouth moved along the soft curve of her throat, exploring the tender slope of her shoulders before dropping light tormenting kisses against the curves of her breasts.

Chloe reached for him instinctively, eyes closed, head thrown back in unaware abandon as her fingers probed the bones of his shoulders, tracing the outline of his spine before curving possessively into the thick dark hair growing low against his nape.

Not even the sudden removal of his body warmth from her, the sudden tensing of his arms as he levered himself upwards, infiltrated the passion-drugged haze engulfing her, and it was only the coolly incisive sound of his voice that finally pierced her fragile bubble of self-delusion, as he grasped her shoulders and pulled her towards him, forcing her face round so that she was forced to witness her own reflection in the mirrored wardrobe opposite the bed.

'Take a good look, Chloe,' he said cruelly, 'and admit that you're a hypocrite. You married me for money and position, you told Marisa. I don't do a thing for you physically and never did. Just take a good look at yourself and repeat that statement to me—if you can!'

Chloe was mortified. She drew a shuddering breath, trying to avert her eyes from her reflection and yet completely unable to do so, mesmerised by the sight of her aroused body, the taut thrust of her breasts, the swollen outline of her mouth, her tangled hair, the silken sheen to her body, all familiar and yet so unfamiliar in this, an openly wanton pose.

'Please. . . .'

The word was a shaky whisper, but it seemed that even now, having witnessed her humiliation, Leon had not drunk his cup of revenge to the full.

'Please what?' he goaded. 'Please leave you alone? Please don't force you to accept the truth? Please take tonight to its ultimate conclusion and make love to you; possess you completely, even though, according to you, I never once, in the boring months of our marriage, managed to arouse the slightest desire in you?'

His voice so husky, shivering across her nerves, hardened over the last words, and Chloe closed her eyes, trying to blot out his features and the sick knowledge of what Marisa had done. And yet hadn't he injured her far more than she was supposed to have injured him? He complained that she had married him for money—and yet hadn't he married her for even less worthy reasons, and not expected her to protest?

But of course one had to take into account his male pride; that fiery Greek pride which made him demand love from her even while he was not prepared to give the same to her. And he called her a hypocrite!

'Oh, don't worry,' Leon continued in that same hateful cold voice, 'I fully intend to possess you, Chloe—that is the whole purpose of the exercise— but first I wanted to remind you past all forgetting that no matter what you may feel about me mentally, physically you want me. Don't you?' he demanded, reinforcing his argument by winding the silky length of her hair through his fingers and tightening them into it until she cried out in mingled pain and shame as she saw again the pale, glimmering outline of her body.

'Just as you want me,' she retaliated, driven to make some response.

'Just as I want you,' Leon agreed sombrely. 'And how I want you right at this minute!' His warm breath touched her skin, her pulses racing in sudden urgent desire, her body responding instantly to the smoky desire lacing the bitter words.

'*Cristos*, Chloe!'

Perspiration broke out on her skin, her body shaking feverishly as he bent his head, tracing its slender outlines with hands and lips which drove her from anger to an ever-growing need, her own lips rediscovering the pleasures of his flesh. The buckle of his trousers impeded the downward caress of her fingers, her impatient fumblings brushed aside with a muttered oath as Leon disposed of the unwanted barrier himself, and at last there was nothing to come between the heated warmth of their flesh. Leon's hands rested lightly on the tenderness of her stomach before moving upwards to cup and linger over her breasts, his own stomach muscles clenching involuntarily as Chloe followed the downward arrowing path of dark hairs, from the breadth of his chest to the taut flatness of his belly, before they were removed and desire exploded between them with the fierce intensity of a funeral pyre, burning away bitterness and anger and leaving only the pure brilliant flame of their mutual need.

The past, the future, both ceased to exist. There was only now, and the fierce, tumultuous clamouring of feelings kept too long in check. It was like a symphony played with instruments perfectly in tune and perfectly attuned to one another until it seemed to Chloe, hazily suspended somewhere between heaven and earth in the aftermath of their lovemaking, that life could hold no more perfect pleasure.

Reflections of water dancing on the ceiling, translucent and unfamiliar, woke Chloe from the depths of a dreamless sleep. She turned her head and saw the cup of tea at the side of the bed. Realisation dawned. She turned her head to the left, to where Leon lay beside her, still asleep, lying on his stomach, his face pillowed on his arm. Pain filled her, so intense that for several minutes it blotted out everything else. How could she have allowed Leon to make love to her! Allowed. She almost groaned out loud. Allowed was just not the word. Encouraged, uninhibitedly enticed; these were better descriptions, she acknowledged in heartsick admission of her own part in what had taken place. She slid out of bed, careful not to wake Leon, and grimaced in distaste as the ruins of her evening dress. What on earth was she going to put on?

'You'll find your clothes in the wardrobe!'

She whirled round, her eyes widening and shadowing with shame and dismay as she faced Leon. He was lying, propped up on one elbow, unashamedly studying the naked length of her body. Just for a second his eyes rested on the faint beginnings of bruises where passion had overridden tenderness.

'I had them brought aboard when I guessed what you were trying to do.'

He frowned suddenly, throwing back the bedclothes and shrugging on the robe lying on the chair beside the bed, coming towards her. Chloe badly wanted to turn her back and walk away, but somehow she simply couldn't, and to her shame tears filmed her eyes, trembling on the lashes she lowered to hide them.

'Tears?' The word was almost a caress. 'Why, I wonder? Regret for what might have been, or shame for what was?'

Chloe shook her head without speaking, gasping as Leon placed his hands very gently against her stomach, the gesture wholly sensual and yet at the same time protective.

'Has it occurred to you that even now my seed might be growing inside you?' he demanded huskily, his eyes darkening. 'Chloe, Chloe, we could have so much together . . . our child . . . children. . . .'

'Everything in fact but love,' Chloe responded lightly, trying not to let her voice shake. 'I. . . .'

'No, don't say anything, unless it is that you agree that we should spend these next few days as though we were indeed making a fresh start. We can do it, Chloe . . . we must do it, for the sake of the child you will bear me.'

Chloe swayed, more tempted than she wanted to admit. She loved him more if anything, not less, and what he was offering her was more, so much more than so many women had, but did she have the courage, the endurance to close her mind to his affair with Marisa and instead concentrate on being the wife he used to shield his half-sister; the woman who stood at his side in public, if not in private; the mother of his children.

'Chloe?'

'Leon, I. . . .'

'*Cristos!* Did I do this?' he demanded suddenly, his

thumb gently brushing the swollen curve of her mouth. 'Did I hurt you? Come, let me see. . . .'

She could no more resist him in this absurdly tender mood than she could fly, Chloe admitted, allowing him to part the soft flesh of her mouth to examine the raw flesh within, still stinging and uncomfortable.

'Shall I kiss it better?'

Beneath the light question Chloe sensed a deeper meaning, and knew without words that it encompassed not just the obvious meaning and that her assent would be taken as an assent to his proposal that they give their marriage a second chance. But dared she? Leon talked about their mutual desire being enough, but if he should discover that she felt more than desire for him; or if she herself found she could not cope with her jealousy of Marisa.

'Surely what we have between us is worth some effort?' Leon asked her.

She opened her mouth, intending to tell him that much as she wished she could, she could not agree; could not commit herself to a future which she knew already held untold pain and despair, but instead to her dismay she heard her own voice, shaky and unfamiliar, saying;

'Yes.'

For a second Leon said nothing, and then he smiled, gently touching his lips to Chloe's before saying softly:

'I am glad that our son is to have both his parents—and now, let us forget everything but the mutual pleasure of rediscovering one another.' He glanced towards the bathroom, and then back at Chloe, picking her up in his arms and striding towards the rumpled bed. 'And the best place to do that is right here.'

CHAPTER SEVEN

IT was late morning before Chloe woke up again, and this time she was alone in the huge bed. She moved luxuriously beneath the silk sheets, her body relaxed and lethargic with the aftermath of love. As she slipped out of bed and pulled on a robe her own reflection caught her eye. How great a difference twenty-four hours could make! Yesterday she had been a pale, unhappy shadow of the woman who stared back at her from the mirror today. Love had effected an almost miraculous transformation. But not mutual love, a small inner voice warned her. She was the one who loved. Leon merely allowed her to give him her love, while he. . . .

She clenched her hands into tiny, desperate fists. No, she mustn't think about Marisa; mustn't spoil what Leon had whispered to her this morning would be their second honeymoon, she must think positive. Who knew, perhaps in time she might be able to win him away from Marisa; perhaps might even already have done so, if she hadn't run away from him—and the unacceptable facts of his relationship with Marisa. She mustn't think of that. She must hold fast to the fact that he wanted *her*, desired *her*; that together they would build a stable family unit; the two of them and their children. He would surely see then that he could not continue his relationship with Marisa?

Deep down inside her Chloe knew that Marisa would not be so easily dislodged from Leon's life. The younger girl was fanatically obsessed with her half-brother, and Chloe shivered, despite the warmth of the stateroom. Fanatics were dangerous people, capable of doing anything to further their cause. Her hands went to her stomach, pain tightening her mouth. Somehow she would have to make Leon believe that Marisa and not she had been responsible for her miscarriage. What was past was past, but she wasn't prepared to run the risk of the same thing happening again.

She stood still, staring into space. The last twenty-four hours had indeed worked a transformation! Here she was not only accepting the fact of resuming her marriage, but actively planning ahead to protect the very life she had sworn to Leon she would never willingly conceive, but then Leon, when he was as attentive and charming as he had been this morning—as it had been when she first met him, was a force to be reckoned with, and one she could not withstand. The love she had thought dead had merely been in hibernation, and the warm heat of the Aegean sun had brought it into full, sensuous life.

'Hey, sleepyhead, are you going to join me for lunch?'

She scurried into the bathroom as Leon strolled into the stateroom, firmly closing and locking the door. Despite her love for him, despite the fact that they had been married and lived together as man and wife, she was still affected by sudden attacks of shyness, and safely behind the locked door, she blushed a little to recall the manner in which Leon had removed her from this very sanctuary only a matter of hours before.

'I'm just getting dressed,' she called out to him. 'I won't be long.'

'Good, Santos is ready to serve lunch. Lobster salad, followed by chocolate soufflé—I remembered your sweet tooth.'

Even with the door between them, Chloe could hear the indulgent amusement in his voice. Really, she thought, exasperated by the way her fingers refused to obey her commands to hurry, anyone would think she was a schoolgirl being 'treated' by a favourite uncle—or an older brother! She froze, paling suddenly, and as though the changed quality of her silence reached him Leon asked her if she was all right.

'Fine. . . .'

Her fingers shook as she slipped on clean under-clothes—Leon had overlooked nothing in his pre-parations, and she had found casual clothes, under-wear, and even a couple of formal evening dresses hanging in the stateroom's generous wardrobes.

She must stop thinking about Marisa. She must put the other girl right out of her mind.

Shelving the problem instead of solving it, a small voice warned her. What she ought to do was tackle Leon and demand to know what he intended to do about Marisa, but she acknowledged that she simply did not have the courage, because she was afraid to hear the truth; afraid to hear that Leon had no inten-tion of giving up his relationship with his half-sister. Was she so weak, she asked herself bitterly, did she honestly have the endurance to simply bury her head in the sand and pretend that Marisa didn't exist?

But Leon had tried to arrange a marriage for Marisa, a more hopeful voice reminded her; surely that proved something?

Any number of things, Chloe acknowledged

grimly. It could simply mean that he realised that he could not keep the affair a secret for ever. His marriage to her had been the first step in trying to deflect attention from Marisa—the other girl was so emotional, so possessive that he must surely live in fear of her blurting out the truth during a temper tantrum— perhaps his attempt to find a marriage partner for Marisa had just been a second step in the same direction. However, Marisa had defeated him, and would continue to defeat him, Chloe reflected. It was true that the younger girl did not know yet that the Kriticos family had had second thoughts and withdrawn from the match, but Chloe could see a procession of possible bridegrooms being treated to a similar display of unpleasant behaviour, until Leon gave up; after all, he could surely not want to see her married to someone else. Leon had a possessive streak which she herself had witnessed only this morning, when for all his tenderness there had been a hint of finely controlled violence beneath the hands which had coaxed her body into urgent, delighted life.

When she stepped on to the sun-deck fifteen minutes later, Chloe found Leon waiting beneath a gaily striped awning, while a steward set covered dishes down on an attractively decorated table.

'Ah, there you are.' Leon stood up lazily, sunlight glinting on the dark hairs sprinkling muscled tanned legs, brief white shorts and a thin cotton knitted top his only covering. In comparison Chloe felt overdressed in her pretty pink and white cotton skirt with its matching camisole top and toning short-sleeved jacket. Leon appraised her for so long that she started to fidget, wondering what he was looking at, her fingers going anxiously to the hair she had just combed.

'Is . . . is there something wrong?' she demanded breathlessly at last.

Leon's lazy smile curled the corners of his mouth in open appreciation.

'On the contrary,' he told her huskily, coming towards her and escorting her to the table. 'Everything is most definitely right, apart from the fact that you're a little overdressed.'

He laughed to see her flush and glance indignantly at the steward, and shook his head.

'Santos does not speak English. Did you enjoy your rest?' He was laughing again, and Chloe tried hard to appear coolly confident. 'Oh, very well,' he drawled when she refused to speak. 'I shall stop teasing you, although it is delightful to see the pretty colour rising so betrayingly in your cheeks. Come, we shall eat lunch, then after we have rested, we shall stop the yacht and swim. There is nothing quite like swimming in the open sea. You will love it.' He leaned over nibbling her throat sensuously while his hand rested warm and vibrant against her rib-cage. 'Are you sure you want lunch, my Chloe?' he demanded huskily against her neck. When she quivered betrayingly in his arms, Leon smiled into her eyes. 'Tonight we shall dine by starlight, alone together, drifting through seas only several shades darker than your eyes after I have made love to you.'

'It sounds almost too romantic to be true,' Chloe interrupted, striving for a light, careless note, and failing dismally as her voice betrayed her, shaking a little, her lips parting in mute pleading as she looked at Leon.

'Don't do that,' Leon warned softly, leaning forward to part her lips with a tanned thumb. 'You'll make me forget all about lunch, and Santos won't like that.'

'Well, we had better sit down, then,' Chloe replied demurely, joining in the game. 'I don't want to upset Santos.'

'I knew you'd say that!' Leon groaned, pulling out an attractive wrought iron chair with a cushion patterned in fresh greens and white. 'Spoilsport!'

Subsiding into the chair, Chloe felt herself beginning to relax; Leon in this mood was irresistible, and she couldn't remember ever seeing him like this before, not even on their honeymoon.

The lobster salad was delicious, and although she hadn't been aware of much breeze coming off the sea, Chloe reflected that it must be the fresh air which was responsible for her suddenly hearty appetite; that and her sudden determination to put yesterday and tomorrow out of her mind and concentrate simply on today.

She glanced towards Leon. The sun glinted on the gold of his wedding ring. He refilled her glass, and when Chloe reached for it, his fingers interlinked with hers on the table, cupping and lifting the glass to her lips.

'To us,' he toasted softly. 'To us and a fresh start, a fresh life together.'

'Without Marisa?' The question trembled on her lips, but was swallowed with the cool dry white wine to lodge uncomfortably against her heart, and so she contented herself with a twisted little smile, as she echoed Leon's toast, the glass cool against her sunwarmed lips. This was definitely the life, she reflected half an hour later, stretched out at Leon's side on a sunlounger, her head pillowed on her shoulder as she relaxed with the easy motion of the yacht. Leon had already explaining that the yacht was an ocean-going vessel, capable of swift speed and complete with all the latest radar and technological devices. Chloe had shivered a little when he had described to her the fate suffered by some friends of his off Bermuda the previous summer. Their vessel had been hijacked and they had been cast adrift in an inflatable dinghy, from which they had been lucky to be rescued twelve hours later.

The authorities had been laconic in the face of their fear and anger. Such incidents were commonplace, and the stolen vessels were used for drug smuggling, and Leon's friends had been told that they were lucky to be alive; many other people had been killed, or left to die slowly of thirst and starvation. Seeing Chloe shiver, Leon assured her that nothing similar was likely to happen to them. He pulled her to her feet, to show her over the yacht, and Chloe marvelled at its luxurious appointments. There were two staterooms, and four cabins; a room which Leon used as a study-cum-library, a dining room furnished as elegantly as any possessed by a stately home, and a drawing room, so palatial that Chloe caught her breath in awe.

'I bought it as a mobile conference suite,' Leon explained to her. 'It saves time to be able to conduct business meetings while travelling, and while some people prefer private jets, we of the Aegean have a love of the sea which is with us from birth.

'How about a swim?' he suggested when their tour was completed. 'I shall tell the captain to drop anchor.'

'Sounds lovely!' Chloe enthused, already imagining the cool, silky feel of the water on her skin. 'I'll just go and change into a swimsuit.'

Leon's eyebrows shot up in amusement, his voice deepening as he asked, 'Why bother? The men will not see us, if that's what's worrying you. There is nothing like the feel of the sea against one's flesh— the ultimate freedom. Very well,' he sighed when Chloe continued to look doubtful, 'Get your suit, then, my little prude.'

Chloe could not find a swimsuit, but she did find several bikinis, all so minuscule and brief that they widened her eyes in bemusement.

In the end she chose a pretty lemon one, really nothing more than the briefest triangle of cotton fastening over the hips with pert bows and a twist of lemon which did almost nothing to conceal her breasts. There was a matching cotton shirt to wear over it and Chloe pulled it over her head, hurrying up on to the deck.

The motion of the yacht had changed, and from cleaving the dense blue of the sea, it now bobbed up and down gently on the slow swell. A ladder had been dropped over the side of the vessel into the water, and a diving platform fastened in place. On the table where they had enjoyed their lunch now stood a tall jug of fresh fruit juice, and Leon was lazing in a chair, drinking a glass of it. He looked up as Chloe approached, his eyes appraising her slender shape. He himself had the physique of an Olympic athlete, muscles tautening beneath the satin skin as he stood up to relieve her of her robe.

'Yes,' he murmured softly as he looked at her, 'I had forgotten that you were no longer a girl.' His fingers slid over her rib-cage to cup the full softness of one breast, amusement glinting in his eyes as hers widened. 'Another few centimetres and you might as well not be wearing this,' he murmured in her ear. 'I don't know which is the more erotic—imagining you without it, or seeing you in it.'

'I thought we were going to swim,' Chloe reminded him primly, shielding her eyes from the bright glare of the sun. In the distance she could just about make out the soft, humped outline of several small islands. 'Which ones are they?' she asked Leon curiously. Long before she had ever met him she had dreamed of coming to the Aegean; of seeing for herself the wild beauty of its islands, and the haunting loveliness of its sea, so gentle in this mood, and yet so dangerous when the winds of the *meltemi* whipped it into a furious aggressor, menacing both man and land.

'They are Ios, Paros and Naxos,' Leon told her. 'We shall be sailing between Ios and Santorini. It is on Ios that Homer is said to be buried, and his tomb is there. We could visit it if you wish, perhaps dine there tomorrow?'

'I should like that,' Chloe agreed, glancing across to the islands, veiled in lilac blue mists. No wonder the Greeks had been such storytellers, such poets; with so much beauty all around them how could it be any different?

'Remember not to swim too far from the yacht,' he added warningly. 'Distances can be deceptive.'

'Don't worry—I enjoy swimming, but I've no ambitions to join the Olympic class! Not that I could anyway,' she admitted ruefully.

Unlike Leon, she acknowledged several seconds later, watching him cleave the water with breathtaking speed and economy of movement. Of course a man raised in Greece would be found to love the water—he had said as much himself, but watching him, the effortless propulsion through the water, the sleek, tanned skin, Chloe knew that she was watching him in his element.

'Come on in!' he shouted to her, floating on his back and watching her scramble down the metal ladder. Not for Chloe a spectacular dive into the dense blue sea. It was all right for Leon to laugh at her, she thought crossly, gingerly releasing her hold of the safely solid ladder, she wasn't a creature of the sea!

That Leon most definitely was he proceeded to demonstrate, swimming round and under her, surfacing at her side, and playfully ducking her beneath the waves, teasing her with a speed which left no room for retaliation.

'Brute!' she shouted at one point, when she had been tugged beneath the waves for the umpteenth time. 'It's not fair. You're far too good!'

'That's the first time a woman's ever told me that,' Leon murmured throatily, grasping a handful of her hair, the silver strands floating round them like pale seaweed. His hands slid from her hair to her shoulders, and down to her waist, moulding her against him, while he supported them both, and Chloe realised with a sudden shock of recognition that, true to his word, Leon was swimming without anything on!

'Chloe!' The teasing was gone from his voice, her name an urgent whisper on lips that claimed hers, salty and warm as they explored the inner softness of her mouth. The gentle tug on the tiny bows securing her bikini went unnoticed as she gave herself up to the sweet seduction of Leon's kiss, and it was only when his hands slid upwards to cup and caress her breasts that she realised what he had done.

'That's better,' Leon murmured huskily. 'Now you do look like a sea nymph come to life.'

After the first initial strangeness Chloe was forced to admit that there was something undeniably pleasurable about the feel of the cool water against her skin; about the hitherto unknown freedom her body was delighting in; about the teasing, silky brush of Leon's skin against hers as he pursued her mock-threateningly through the waves; the game, so innocent on the surface, was in actuality a slow and erotic arousal of senses steadily inflamed by the touch and knowledge of each other's proximity.

Leon seemed to know instinctively when Chloe began to tire, and guided her easily back towards the stationary vessel. When she hovered anxiously at the foot of the ladder he grinned understandingly, 'Okay, sea nymph, I'll go up first and throw you down a towel.'

Chloe knew that she was perhaps being silly; Leon had already said that they could not be seen, but even so, she had an entirely British reticence about clambering nude on to the deck, with the same careless panache that Leon had managed to achieve.

He was beautiful, she thought irrelevantly, watching him stride towards her and kneel on the deck to proffer the protection of a towelling robe, if such an adjective could be applied to anything as intensely male as his powerfully muscled body.

She was grateful for the drink he had poured her. The salt had made her thirsty and she drank almost

greedily, lying back in her reclining chair, surprised
to discover how tired the brief exercise had left her.
She was out of condition, she thought, but then her
present life-style left no time for such self-indulgent
pastimes as swimming and sunbathing.

Leon lay down at her side, head pillowed on his
arms.

'Another drink?'

Chloe shook her head. She felt the engines start up
beneath them and glanced enquiringly at him.

'We'll drop anchor in Ios harbour tomorrow afternoon, and go ashore for dinner later.' He frowned
suddenly. 'I wish my father had lived to do this. It
was his life's ambition to sail these seas, and explore
the islands, but it was one he was never able to realise.
There was always something more important, like
sending me to school, and finding husbands for his
sisters. You would have liked him,' he told Chloe.
'He was a simple man in many ways; a very honest
and upright man who believed in the power of hard
work. He believed in it so much that he eventually
killed himself,' Leon added soberly while Chloe
listened to him in silence. Leon had never talked to
her about his family before, and a feeling of tender
warmth filled her as she listened to him, her hand
going out to touch his bronzed forearm in a gesture of
sympathy that brought a brief smile to his lips.

'Everything I am I owe to him. Without the edu-
cation he scrimped and scraped to give me I would
never have been what I am today. My very first
business venture was financed by him. If I am half
the father he was I shall think I have done well. He
entrusted Marisa to me when he died. Her mother,
Lydia, was the nearest thing I had ever known to a

mother. My father married her when I was eight—my own mother died when I was born, and between them I suppose he and Lydia spoilt me shamefully.'

Chloe felt her heart sink. Leon would never give up Marisa in favour of her; he was bound too closely to her. Ice-cold fingers touched her spine, the brightness of the sun suddenly dimmed as though by an unseen cloud.

'I know Marisa can be . . . awkward, but. . . .'

'There's no need to say any more. I understand,' Chloe stopped him brightly. Please, God, don't let her have to listen to Leon explaining just why he loved Marisa so much today. Today was hers, and she refused to share it with the other girl's shadow. 'Tell me about when you were a little boy.'

'What is there to tell? I was obnoxious, as most small boys are, and no doubt often hurt my parents with my arrogance and youth, as children do. Perhaps my punishment is that neither of them lived to see me become the success they had always hoped I would be. Lydia died when Marisa was two, and my father followed her only a handful of months later.'

For a moment both of them were silent. His words had given Chloe a deeper insight into his love for Marisa, but that didn't stop jealousy searing her whenever she thought of the other girl.

'You'd better get something on your skin,' Leon said abruptly, changing the subject. 'You're so fair you're bound to burn. The breeze off the sea is deceptive, and unless you want to be badly sunburned I suggest you get something on it right away. Stay here,' he told her. 'I'll get something.'

He pulled on his shorts, standing up as he did so,

and as she watched him a lump came into Chloe's throat. How could she ever have thought that she had stopped loving him? Love didn't die simply because one refused to acknowledge its existence, especially not a love like hers; it was imprinted on her heart, scorched into her flesh, indelibly written into her senses.

When Leon left she turned on her stomach, shielding her eyes from the sun, which had now started to dip towards the horizon. She had an odd, childish desire to hold back its descent to stop time, as though somehow the coming of the hours of darkness harboured some nameless evil. The legacy of childhood nightmares, she told herself, trying not to admit that her fears went deeper than that and owed their existence to the knowledge that sooner or later she would have to face up to the truth—but not yet, an inner voice pleaded. Not yet!

'I'll do your back for you.'

She hadn't heard Leon approach, and jumped as he spread the cool ointment on her skin, relaxing as his fingers spread out and gently massaged the cream into her back. The slow, rhythmic caress of his hands, at first relaxing, soon became unwittingly erotic, and Chloe had to repress the desire to turn over and press her body into the hard warmth of his.

A delicious languor washed over her, making her as supine as a cat caressed to the point of blissful purring, her body unconsciously sensual. Her senses heightened to a point where she was vividly aware of everything around her, she could feel the pulsating desire pounding through her in an insistent tide, her breasts hard and swollen, echoing the growing ache deep down inside her. Leon's hands moved downwards, sliding her arms completely free of her brief robe, her body exulting with fierce pleasure as his hands rested on her waist.

'Leon!'

His name sounded thick and blurred on her tongue, her body quivering as he turned her over very slowly.

For several seconds he did nothing but look down at her, but as though the Greek sun had aroused something pagan inside her, Chloe felt no embarrassment, instead exulting in the slow, burning intensity of eyes that examined every inch of her body with such open desire that her stomach contracted protestingly with the intensity of her own response. To be so close, within touching distance, and yet not touched; to feel the heat coming off Leon's skin and know her own body ached to feel that burning heat, aroused her to a peak of desire so intense that it was almost unbearable. Leon lowered his head and she stretched out her arms towards him, but he captured them, pinioning them above her head. The brief brush of his lips against her was like the merest sip of water to someone dying of thirst, a small moan of protest was torn from her throat as his mouth left hers.

'Leon!' She made no attempt to hide her feelings, her eyes the colour of pansies as they pleaded mutely with him, and then his mouth was on her skin, arousing, satisfying, encouraging and feeding the desire which seemed to pour through her in a red-hot tide, his name sobbed from her lips as he kissed the smooth warmth of her throat, the twin peaks of her breasts, swollen and hard beneath the hot rasp of his tongue.

Leon's breathing was as ragged as her own when he lifted his head and said jerkily, 'This time you will be with me every step of the way; for once you will

cast aside that prim British manner which always
withholds something from me and you will want me
with a need as deep as mine for you.'

He released her hands and Chloe reached for him,
her fingers curling into his hair, tugging his head
downwards, her senses drinking in the scent and feel
of him. His tongue traced the outline of her lips, hot
and dry beneath its sensual torment, her hands sliding
down the muscled breadth of his back to caress the
narrow waist and sleekly male hips until the all too
brief kisses with which Leon was tormenting her lips
swept aside the last remnants of her self-control and
her hands grasped the thick dark hair at the nape of
his neck, holding his mouth to her own.

'At last!' she heard Leon mutter thickly. 'At last
my sea nymph becomes human!'

Chloe felt as though she were drowning, melting,
being absorbed into Leon's body, as though she
wanted this kiss, with all its searing heat, to go on for
ever, as though the only thing which would ever make
her complete was Leon's possession. The taut,
throbbing pressure of his thighs made her ache for
appeasement, her body arching invitingly beneath
the heated thrust of his, her nails raking the lean,
tanned back as he finally possessed her with an
urgency that brought fierce cries of pleasure to the
lips she pressed against his skin, her tongue tasting
the sweat beading his throat as the muscles corded
with the compulsion that seized them both.

When it was over Leon refused to let her out of his
arms.

'At last I have truly possessed you,' he said thickly
against her throat. 'At last you are actually mine.'

He carried her down to their stateroom and slept

with his head pillowed against her breasts, the graze of his breath against her skin a shadowy reminder of how, earlier, that very same breath had aroused her to the point where nothing mattered except that he possess her.

CHAPTER EIGHT

LEON was in the shower when Chloe woke up. She was dismayed to realise that she must have slept right through dinner—and this was confirmed when Leon walked into the room, pulling on jeans as he did so. He walked over to the bed and kissed her mouth before touching the flushed peaks of her breasts with gentle lips.

'Today I shall show you Ios, and tonight we shall dine at a restaurant I know. It is owned by friends of mine, but first I have some calls to make.' When Chloe looked surprised he smiled. 'But naturally we have ship-to-shore communication, and apparently some of my associates were trying to get in touch with me yesterday. Fortunately I had given orders to the crew that we were not to be disturbed.' He laughed when Chloe flushed. 'Ah, your eyes reproach me for being so ungentlemanly as to remind you of our mutual passion, but your body rebels against them. And besides . . .' his voice dropped, seductive as melted honey, 'I find it erotic to remember how it was between us, how these . . .' he touched her breasts lightly, 'pleaded my possession, and all of you enticed me into stealing from the gods, if only briefly, their power and divinity. I'll leave you to get dressed,' he added, 'and I'll instruct the crew to drop anchor at Ios. We should be there by lunchtime. We'll eat on board, explore the island, and then have dinner.'

Bearing in mind the fact that they would probably

be walking without any protection from the sun, Chloe applied sun-screen liberally to her face, and found a sun-hat in pretty pink straw to match the soft pink cotton dress she had chosen from the wardrobe. Pink sandals completed the outfit, and the delicate crinkle-pleated cotton floated ethereally around her as she walked up on deck.

The sun shone from a cloudless sky, so blue that it was almost impossible to believe it was real. During the night they had obviously been sailing towards Ios, and now they were at anchor just outside the harbour and while Chloe waited for Leon to join her she was able to amuse herself watching the various comings and goings amongst the many craft.

Shops and houses clustered around the harbour interspersed with tavernas and bars, holidaymakers thronging the pavements and roads. Chloe was engrossed in watching them when Leon came up on deck, the warmth of his fingers on her neck making her turn to smile up at him.

They had chicken breast cooked in wine and served with tiny mushrooms and crispy fresh salad. Afterwards Chloe barely had room for the fresh fruit salad. Leon, she noticed, did not have any sweet, apparently preferring a wedge of Stilton and crackers.

'A taste I developed when I stayed with a business acquaintance in London for several months,' he explained, seeing Chloe's surprise. 'Would you care for some?'

Chloe shook her head, patting her stomach. 'I've eaten too much already,' she admitted ruefully. 'I can see that I'm going to have to get to work on my will power!'

It was a tacit admission that she was willing to stay with him, and Leon's glance strayed over her slender figure, coming to rest on her face as he raised her fingers to his lips, kissing them individually and holding them within his grasp for a few seconds.

'You won't regret it,' he said huskily at last. 'And now, let me show you Ios.'

It was an afternoon that Chloe felt would live on in her memory for ever. They strolled along the harbour hand in hand, her heart swelling with pride whenever she glanced at Leon's tall, lean frame. Even dressed casually in a thin short-sleeved shirt and jeans he had an aura of power about him that turned heads—especially female ones, as Chloe wasn't slow to notice. She herself was not short of admiring male glances and more than one dark-eyed Greek looked enviously at first at Leon and then at Chloe's silver fairness.

They spent the early afternoon exploring the tiny alleyways off the harbour. Leon obviously knew the island well and led Chloe unerringly to a tiny shop set in a row of whitewashed houses, its shutters closed against the heat of the sun.

The door opened to Leon's knock and a weather-beaten face peered round the door, breaking into a beaming smile as Leon said teasingly, 'Ari! I thought perhaps you had forgotten me!'

A stream of Greek was the man's response as he stood back to allow them to step down into the small shop. The stone-cobbled floor felt blissfully cool after the heat of the pavement, although it took some time for Chloe's eyes to grow accustomed to the swift change from brilliant sunshine to half-light. The two men were still talking; or rather the old man was talking and Leon was listening, and Chloe stared round the shop with curious eyes. It obviously sold fishermen's supplies of all types, and the smell of tar mingled pungently with the tang of salt.

'So,' the old man said at last, turning to Chloe and studying her. 'You have found her and brought her to me at last? You have chosen well,' he said to Leon, 'and they will become her as they could never become a woman of our race; her skin will reflect their radiance. I shall get them.' He saw that Chloe was looking increasing puzzled and explained in careful English:

'Many years ago your husband came to this island after a bad storm. In that storm I had lost my boat and my son, and I was on the point of despair. It was your husband who gave me new hope, who reminded me that I had a daughter and would one day have grandsons. He also gave me the money to buy and stock this shop, and although I have never ceased to mourn my son I have come to realise that life is always worth living. As your husband predicted, I have two fine grandsons, neither of whom will ever need to brave the sea for their living. In repayment of all that your husband had done I offered him the only thing of value I owned—a string of pearls given to me by my father, who dived for them in these very seas. Your husband refused. I was to keep the pearls, he told me, and only when he found a woman worthy of such a gift would he come to claim them from me. For many years I have feared that they would never be claimed, but now that I see you I see that he was wise to wait.'

He disappeared into the rear of the shop, and Chloe turned impulsively to Leon, her voice husky with emotion as she tried to put her feelings into words.

'He is right,' Leon told her softly. 'Until now there has never been a woman whom I considered worthy of the pearls, whose value can be termed in the number of lives sacrificed in obtaining them. Diving for pearls used to be the only way a man of these islands could ever hope to amass any true wealth. What Ari didn't tell you was that his father and three of his uncles lost their lives without completing a single strand of pearls. Ari himself dived for the remaining four, and permanently damaged his lungs in doing so. They weight themselves with rocks and dive to almost unimaginable depths.'

Before Chloe could comment Ari was back, a small leather box clutched in one gnarled hand. He gave it to Leon, who flicked the catch with his thumb. The lid flew back and Chloe caught her breath in awe.

The pearls seemed to glow with vibrant life. She touched them reverently, loving their warm, supple texture.

'Turn round.'

She did as Leon instructed, closing her eyes as she felt him slide the single strand of pearls round her throat, and secure the fastening.

'Well, Ari?'

The old man smiled.

'As I said,' he reiterated simply, 'you have chosen well, my friend, and I am glad to have discharged a debt which has sometimes lain heavily upon me.'

They remained with him another half hour, drinking strong Turkish coffee, Chloe listening while the two men reminisced. It was after three when they finally left, stepping out into a sunshine whose brilliance shocked.

There was one thing which puzzled Chloe as they

sauntered towards the taxi rank to secure a car to take them to see Homer's tomb, and when they emerged from the alleyway into the square she asked Leon curiously, 'Why did you accept the necklace— Oh, I know it's beautiful, but . . .'

'It was the only thing of any real value he had apart from his shop,' Leon supplied for her. 'Chloe, you still have a lot to learn about the Greek male. Ari was glad of my help at the time he needed it, but he wanted to repay me, and the only way he could do that was by offering me his most valuable possession. Had I refused it, or worse still, intimated that I could have easily bought the same thing from a jeweller, he would have been mortally offended, you must see that? To have refused would have seemed as though I didn't value the sacrifice he was making; the sacrifices which had gone into obtaining those pearls. Now do you see?'

Chloe did. He was a strange mixture, this man she had married; as tender and caring as the most perceptive of women at times, and yet on other occasions. . . . She shivered suddenly and glanced up at the sky, wondering if the cool breeze was just her imagination. She had to try to put the past behind her. But it wouldn't stay buried for ever. For the sake of the child she might one day bear Leon, she would have to talk to him about Marisa, about his plans. But not yet, a cowardly voice pleaded. Let me have today!

It was all too easy to give in to it. There *was* a cool breeze, Chloe was sure, she felt it again as Leon hailed an ancient taxi for them, but when she glanced up towards him, he seemed unaware of the sudden chill of the air. Once inside the taxi, Chloe forgot about it. They drove along a narrow road, past freshly painted windmills towards the spot where the great historian, who had for so many centuries been maligned merely as a story-teller, and who had given the world the epic and detailed history of valour and retribution in the *Iliad* and the *Odyssey* lay buried. How Chloe had loved tragic Achilles; had wept for Cassandra, cursed by Apollo with the gift of prophecy; had exulted with Penelope, rewarded for her faithful diligence by the return of her husband.

The burial place was not as impressive as Chloe had expected, but nevertheless there was an undeniable timeless sense of peace surrounding it that left her feeling enriched when, after they had stood in mutual silence for several minutes, Leon directed her back towards the taxi.

It was early evening when they returned to the yacht, but for the first time since she had come to Greece there was no spectacular sunset.

Chloe dressed in one of the two evening dresses she had found on board the yacht, a deep vivid pink, emphasising her golden tan, its long skirt sweeping the carpet as she walked over to the mirror. The dress was a slender sheath, the bodice moulding her breasts and embroidered with small pink beads which glittered in the light, without detracting from the subtle shimmer of her pearls. Chloe touched them gently, tears misting her eyes. She had been unbearably touched that the old man had thought her worthy of such a gift. 'I'll live up to them,' she promised him silently, the words a private vow that from somewhere she would find the courage to confront Leon about Marisa.

He came in while she was applying a fine coat of soft pink lipstick, and stood watching her for several seconds without speaking.

'It's not too dressy, is it?' Chloe asked anxiously, indicating her outfit. 'You said a nightclub. . . .'

'It's fine,' Leon assured her. 'By and large the tavernas and bars expect their patrons to dress casually, but this nightclub is attached to a particularly exclusive hotel, patronised by people who prefer to spend their evenings in something other than jeans and tee-shirts. I'm glad you're wearing the pearls,' he added softly, dropping a light kiss on the back of her neck.

Chloe was wearing her hair up, secured by two pretty combs, and as she slipped into her evening sandals she gave her appearance a final cursory inspection. Not perhaps for the catwalk of Monsieur René, but passable nonetheless!

Another decrepit taxi was waiting for them as they went ashore, and despite its battered appearance it was clean and comfortable. Their driver handled his vehicle with a certain careless panache which had Chloe gripping her door on more than one occasion, until Leon slipped his arm round her waist, securing her against him.

It was impossible to see anything of their surroundings in the dark, the faintly ghostly white arms of windmills the only landmarks Chloe could discern, until, at last, down below them in a small bay she could see surf creaming, and the multi-coloured lights illuminating an olive grove.

The taxi screeched to a halt in front of an impressively porticoed entrance. Leon alighted and paid the driver, giving him brief instructions before helping Chloe out of the car.

'I have asked him to pick us up later. My friends

think nothing of dancing until dawn, but I can think of far better ways of passing the night, can't you?'

Chloe was still faintly flushed when they entered the hotel foyer. A beaming waiter addressed a few words in Greek to Leon before hurrying through a door marked 'Private'. A few seconds later it was thrown open again, this time from the other side, and the man who emerged hurried up to Leon, embracing him in a fierce hug.

'Leon! What a pleasure. Why didn't you tell us you were coming?'

'A spur-of-the-moment decision,' Leon replied, giving Chloe a teasing smile. 'Kristos, allow me to introduce you to my wife. . . .'

Kristos Kalymides bowed, and smiled.

'And Marisa?'

'On Eos.'

'Ah well, never mind. You are here, and you will remain as our guests. You wish to play the tables?' When Leon shook his head Kristos smiled. 'Forgive me my friend, of course you do not. I was forgetting, the wheeling and dealing of big business provides more of a test of skill and nerve than the roulette wheel ever could, does it not?'

'I have brought Chloe so that she may see traditional Greek entertainment,' Leon explained. 'Do you still. . . .'

'But of course,' Kristos assured him, without giving him time to finish. 'But not for the tourists, you understand. The men resent performing before such an audience. To them the dance is a serious matter, a sacred action. You will dine here, of course? What would you like? Caviare? I. . . .'

Leon shook his head. 'Nothing like that, Kristos. I

should like Chloe to enjoy some of our traditional Greek food. Soup, such as your mother used to make for me as a boy; pitta baked as only she can; tiny mussels fresh from the sea, kebabs—and then to finish perhaps an almond pastry?'

'Leave it all to me,' Kristos told him, beaming. 'Come, Anthony will show you to a table. Spiro is leading the dancers now. Do you remember him? He used to go out on his father's boat, until the old man died, and now Spiro's brother makes a better living from taking tourists round the bay than his poor father made in a dozen fishing trips. Truly things have changed!'

'You're an old fraud,' Leon grinned. 'What would you do without the tourists, my friend? Who would occupy this fine hotel, eh?'

Kristos laughed, slapping Leon on the back and hailing a waiter who hurried respectfully to his side.

'Enjoy your evening. I hope to be able to join you later, or would I be de trop?'

They were shown to a table right in front of a round dance floor, but at the same time discreetly concealed from the rest of the diners.

Never, outside Paris, had Chloe eaten in such luxurious surroundings.

Leon had taken her to Maxim's to celebrate their engagement, and vastly different though the settings were, in the swift but unflustered movement of the waiters, the discreet glitter of expensive jewellery and the undisputable aura of real wealth, Chloe saw similarities. The soup, which she had faced doubtfully, proved to be delicious, thick and creamy. The tiny mussels which followed were a delicacy which Leon plainly relished. They were given wine, full-bodied with a faintly nutty flavour which went well with their lamb kebabs.

Chloe barely had room for the promised sweet pastry by the time she had finished the succulent pieces of lamb, but to please their host, who had appeared at their table, she forced herself to eat the almost too sweet almond-flavoured delicacy.

Most of the diners had finished eating; the hum of conversation started to die away, and Chloe was aware of a sense of expectation filling the elegant room with its almost stark black and white decor and marble-topped tables.

When the troupe of male dancers finally appeared on the floor the silence thickened. Leon relaxed in his seat, his fingers reaching for and playing with Chloe's.

'What you are about to see is a performance by a nationally acclaimed troupe; they have won prizes all over Greece and Kristos is fortunate in having secured them for his guests.'

Chloe soon realised what he meant. Although she knew next to nothing about the finer points of Greek dancing, she recognised skill when she saw it, and she was seeing it now. She sat on the edge of her seat, breathless with amazement, as she tried to follow the swift steps, her attention wavering only when she saw waiters weaving silently between the tables carrying piles of plates.

'What are they doing?' she whispered to Leon, as people stretched out to take a handful—in some cases two handfuls!

'Wait and see,' Leon teased mysteriously, beckoning a waiter and taking half a dozen himself which he placed on the table at Chloe's side. 'Would you like another drink?'

Chloe shook her head. She was already feeling a little muzzy, and tonight she was determined to face up to Marisa's presence in Leon's life—to face up to it and ask what he intended to do about it, and she needed a clear head for that!

The music reached a wild crescendo; the onlookers came to their feet, and to Chloe's astonishment began to hurl plates towards the dancers, who continued to perform their intricate steps, almost without hesitation.

'What on earth are they doing?' she whispered urgently to Leon.

'It is a sign of their appreciation,' he explained in great amusement. 'The more impressed one is with the dancing the more plates one throws. In Spain they throw flowers, in appreciation of the matador; in Britain all manner of objects are hurled on to football pitches in recognition of a team's skill, but here in Greece we smash plates. Like this!'

Under his encouragement, tentatively at first, and then gradually with more assurance, Chloe hurled her plates towards the dance floor, marvelling at the adroit manner in which the dancers avoided the shards of pottery.

It was late when they left. Kristos had joined them when the dancers left the floor, and he and Leon had spent some considerable time talking over old times. They had worked together for a time in Athens in the offices of a millionaire ship-owner, but at no time had Leon allowed Chloe to feel neglected or left out. His arm had remained around her at all times, his glance straying to her face, as he explained various anecdotes.

'Before you leave you must meet the dancers,' Kristos told them, and Leon and Chloe were ushered backstage to meet the team of charming young men who had performed so well for them.

After that they had to go up to the family's private apartments to meet Kristos' family and to say 'hello' to the two sleepy children who were roused from their beds to greet the godfather they had not seen for quite some time. At last Leon and Chloe left, not in their taxi, but in Kristos' own car. He came out with them to wave them off, glancing frowningly up at the sky. Leon followed his look, as did Chloe, surprised to see that there were no stars.

'That's a bad sign,' Kristos remarked to Leon. 'The temperature has started to drop too.'

'A storm brewing,' Leon agreed.

'Or the *meltemi* coming early.'

Leon seemed deep in thought on the way back to the yacht and once or twice Chloe had to address a comment to him several times before he acknowledged it. What was on his mind? she wondered.

They boarded the yacht in silence and went straight to their stateroom. The first thing Chloe did was to reach for the fastening of the pearls, but it was too intricate for her to manage and she called to Leon, who was in the act of unfastening his shirt, having already discarded his evening jacket. The male scent of him reached out and enveloped Chloe as he bent over her.

'There you are.' He handed her the pearls with a smile, his eyes suddenly darkening slumberously as they probed the shadowy cleft temptingly concealed by the bodice of her dress. 'Did you enjoy yourself tonight?'

'Yes, I did.'

Whether it was the storm brewing outside or the emotions within the room Chloe did not know, but the air seemed to take on an electric sensitivity, desire pulsating between them, so that she knew even before Leon reached for her with a smothered curse what was going to happen.

Her zip was released and she felt the expensive silk gown slide from her body. Leon lifted her free of it, holding her so tightly within the circle of his arm that she could feel the buttons of his shirt pressing into her skin. She reached upwards, palms flat against the starched whiteness of his shirt, his arms slackening at her faintly murmured protest. His shirt was unfastened at the throat, baring the tanned flesh of his chest and the beginnings of the dark covering of hair. Chloe touched her mouth delicately to his skin, tasting the male texture of it, her lips parting moistly and involuntarily, as Leon's hand cupped her breast, caressing it into swollen awareness, his mouth capturing the frantic pulse throbbing in her throat. Desire overwhelmed her as suddenly as a spring tide. She had no idea that the bed was behind her until Leon lowered her on to it, beginning a slow exploration of her yielding flesh which began at her toes and left not one single inch of her a stranger to the touch of his hands and lips.

His embraces were returned with unashamed desire, and Chloe felt him shudder deeply in her arms, the muscles in his thighs taut as a bowstring as her lips followed the downward arrowing of the dark body hair to the flat maleness of his stomach.

His muttered, '*Cristos*, Chloe,' jerked past gritted teeth, his hands hauling her upwards and against the aroused heat of his body as his mouth possessed hers in a kiss that left them both shuddering mindlessly with the full force of their desire.

In the distance Chloe could hear a sound, familiar and intrusive. She tried to blot it out, pressing her body against Leon's, feverishly entwining the slender length of her limbs with the heated power of his, but it was no use; she could feel him moving away.

'The telephone's ringing,' he muttered hoarsely.

'Then let it,' Chloe longed to plead, but Leon was already sitting up, and reaching for the receiver. He listened in silence for several seconds, his face gradually growing grimmer, and Chloe could almost physically feel him withdrawing from her.

'What's happened? What is it?' she demanded when he replaced the receiver and sat staring into the distance, his forearms resting on his knees.

'It's Marisa,' he said sombrely at last. 'She's disappeared. Apparently she went for a walk this afternoon, and hasn't returned. They're searching the island for her. We have to get back.' He reached for the receiver, pressing the buttons decisively. 'Give me the latest weather report, will you, Captain?' he demanded curtly, 'and prepare to return to Eos—as fast as we can.'

He listened for several seconds, frowning, and tapping impatiently on the bedside table, his thoughts so obviously removed from her that Chloe doubted that he was even aware of her presence.

A feeling of intense bitterness swept over her. She had wanted to ask him about his feelings for Marisa— well, now she was seeing for herself exactly what they were. There could be no doubting his concern for the other girl. Only minutes ago he had been on the point of making love to her, and yet now, after one phone call, she was completely forgotten. Pain welled up inside her, and she reached automatically for her robe.

'The weather report is bad,' Leon told her briefly when he had hung up. 'I hope you're a good sailor, because we're heading right for the storm. Ari was right, apparently. The *meltemi* has come early.'

'But won't it be dangerous?' Chloe queried, shivering a little as she remembered stories she had read about the danger of these Aegean storms. In Ancient Greece they used to think they were caused by the wrath of Poseidon, the sea god, and some islands had even made human sacrifices to him to appease that wrath; as she was being sacrificed to Leon's desire for Marisa!

Sickness welled up inside her.

'Surely it can wait until morning?' she protested. 'Surely Marisa can't have gone far? You said they were out looking for her.'

'You don't understand! I have to go back, I have. . . .' Leon broke off, but not before Chloe had seen the determination burning in his eyes, the inward-looking gaze which obliterated everything but his desire to be with the other girl. Very slowly she got to her feet, gathering up her clothes.

'Chloe. . . .' She hesitated. 'I'm sorry, but this is something I have to do. Bear with me, will you?'

Almost against her will Chloe nodded her head slowly, trying to bury the feelings of fear rising up inside her. What was Leon asking her to do? Forgive him for being unable to fight his feelings for Marisa? Wait patiently in the background? It was natural that he should be concerned about his half-sister, she

told herself, she must stop jumping to foolish con-
clusions. Leon wanted *her*. He had told her so; *shown*
her. She must have faith in him. She drew a shaky
breath, filling her lungs with air.

'I'll go and get dressed.'

'Good girl. I'd better go up on deck. It could turn
out to be a very long night!'

CHAPTER NINE

By the time she had dressed in jeans and a serviceable blouse, Chloe had managed to convince herself that she had read more into Leon's natural concern than she need have done. She must learn to stop tormenting herself by imagining things, she remonstrated with herself as she went to look for Leon, and yet still the niggling doubts persisted, the regret that she had not tackled him about Marisa when she had had the opportunity. Only the most insensitive of human beings would choose now to demand a statement of his future intentions, and yet she couldn't help wishing that things had been resolved between them before they returned to Eos.

She found Leon with the Captain. He greeted her with a brief smile, reaching for her arm to steady her as the yacht wallowed suddenly in a deep trough of water.

Already it had grown colder, the wind blowing Chloe's hair back off her face as she stood on the deck.

'I've charted a course, and with luck we'll miss the worst of it,' the Captain was saying to Leon.

Chloe could feel the wind picking up as he spoke, a distinctly rolling motion replacing the yacht's previous swift progress.

'You go down to the cabin, Chloe,' Leon told her. 'You'll be warm and dry down there at least. I'll stay with the Captain.'

She wanted to protest that she would have preferred him to go below with her, but the precious
closeness they had enjoyed earlier seemed to have
vanished, obliterated by the fierce wind whipping up
the surface of the sea.

To Chloe, waiting below, time seemed to drag.
She tried to read one of the books she found on the
study shelves—stories of Greek mythology—but
found it impossible to concentrate. Several times she
longed to go up on deck and plead with Leon to tell
her of his future intentions towards Marisa, but on
each occasion pride stopped her.

The turning of the door handle brought her to her
feet, her smile fading as one of the stewards walked in
carrying a cup of coffee.

Chloe thanked him and sat down again.
Presumably Leon was drinking his coffee up top with
the Captain. She debated the advisability of going to
join them, but a glance through the porthole showed
her seas of such roughness and ferocity that she judged
it wiser to remain where she was.

Four hours after they had first left Ios they were
approaching the small harbour of Eos. Leon came
down to warn Chloe that they were about to arrive.

'Spiro is standing by with the jeep. He'll drop you
off at the house, and. . . .'

'They still haven't found her, then?' Chloe said
bleakly.

Leon shook his head.

'Leon . . .' she reached towards him impetuously,
trying to break through the barrier he seemed to
have retreated behind, her eyes pleading with him
for understanding. 'Let me come with you,' she
urged. 'Please!'

'It's too dangerous. You don't know the island. For God's sake don't look at me like that!' he demanded hoarsely. 'Try to understand, Chloe.'

She turned away so that he wouldn't see the tears in her eyes, seeing in his refusal to take her with him a rejection of her in favour of Marisa, but common sense told her that the most selfish thing she could do now was to give in to an emotional outburst. Her love for Leon rose above her fear and jealousy, and swallowing hard on the painful lump in her throat, she managed to summon a brief smile.

'Good girl!' Cool, salt-fresh lips brushed hers, and then Leon was gone, disappearing in the direction of the crew's quarters. He returned only when they were on the point of docking, dressed in a padded, protective anorak, his expression coolly controlled as he shouted orders to the Captain.

'I told him to make for Piraeus,' he explained to Chloe as they walked along the gangplank. 'The harbour here isn't sheltered enough to provide sufficient safety in a bad storm.' He swore suddenly as the wind drove icy rain into their faces and Chloe winced against him. Her thin dress was already soaked through and clinging to her, but she was determined to do nothing which might later be construed as a pathetic attempt to prevent Leon from going to look for Marisa.

Leon helped her into the jeep in silence, climbing in himself next to Spiro and slamming the door.

As the vehicle was open, Chloe was even damper and colder when they reached the house than she had been when they left the yacht.

During the drive, Leon questioned Spiro quickly, listening intently as the other man described their search for Marisa, his face growing grimmer with every passing second.

'You say she was heading for the cliffs when Petros saw her?' Leon demanded at one point.

'But she is not there now,' Spiro assured him. 'We have searched—both the cliffs and the beach.'

Knowing that Leon was anxious not to waste time, Chloe reached for the door handle the moment the jeep stopped, but she was so numb with cold and damp that her half frozen fingers refused to respond to the commands of her brain, and it was Leon who had to get out and open it for her.

She tried her best to stand up and walk past him, wincing as pins and needles shot through her chilled legs, and thought she had succeeded until Leon cursed suddenly, sweeping her up into his arms and striding towards the door, which was opened immediately they approached.

Chloe barely had time to see much more than the housekeeper's worried face, and Gina's surprised one, as Leon strode past them towards their room.

There was a moment's pause while he opened the door, then kicked it shut behind him before placing Chloe on the bed and disappearing in the direction of the bathroom. She opened her mouth to protest that there was no need for him to delay, and was immediately silenced by the damp folds of her dress as Leon pulled it over her head, enveloping her in the thick warm towel he had brought from the bathroom, and proceeding to rub life and warmth into her chilled body.

'*Cristos!*' he swore at one point. 'My poor Chloe! I had forgotten you had nothing warm to wear.'

Chloe could not reply. His touch was doing much

more than restoring life to numbed limbs; it was reminding her almost unbearably of the desire which
had flamed between them earlier, and to her chagrin
she could feel her body reacting to his touch. That
Leon was aware of it she could not help but realise,
because his hands stilled suddenly, faint colour running up under his tan.

'Chloe,' he muttered thickly, pulling sharply away
from her, groaning suddenly as the towel dropped
away to reveal the contours of her body, his arms
going round her, as his mouth sought for and found
her own in a kiss that left them both trembling with
the onslaught of desire.

'*Cristos*, I have to go,' Leon protested hoarsely,
removing her arms from his neck. 'I have to, Chloe
. . . God knows, I would give almost anything to stay
here with you but, this is something. . . .'

He left while she had her back to him, not trusting
herself to look at him without begging him to stay.

She had just stepped out of the bath when she
heard someone moving about in the outer room.
Slipping on her robe, she found Gina placing a tray
with a bowl of soup and fresh rolls on the table.

'The *kyrios* said you were to have something warm-
ing,' she said shyly, shivering suddenly as she crossed
to the windows, closing the curtains. 'The *meltemi* is
always bad when it comes early. I told the *kyria* it
was not wise to go out, but she would not listen, the
wind affects some people like that, they are unable to
resist its call. Some say the wind is the voice of the
Furies, luring those foolish enough to listen to it to
their death.'

'What nonsense!' Chloe had to fight to keep the
sharpness from her voice. Gina was simply an island

girl and had doubtless been brought up on such stories. 'I'm sorry, Gina,' she apologised gently. 'The wind must be affecting me too.'

'The *kyria* is not to worry,' Gina comforted her. 'The *kyrios* will be safe.'

Some time towards dawn Chloe fell asleep. Urgent voices outside the bedroom woke her and she sat up abruptly, remembering instantly what had happened. She glanced towards the adjacent pillow, but Leon had quite obviously not slept there. Fear pounded through her veins, her mouth dry with an apprehension she was loath to name, as she pushed her feet into mules and hurried towards the door.

Spiro was outside, talking to Gina, and it was apparent from both their expressions that something was wrong.

'My husband,' Chloe begged anxiously. 'Is he. . . .'

'The *kyrios* is fine,' Spiro assured her, 'but the *thespinis* Marisa——' he shook his head doubtfully.

'They still haven't found her?'

'She is found—yes,' Spiro told her, 'but is not so good. She was in a . . . a cave at the bottom of the cliffs, you understand, and because of the sea had been trapped there. The *kyrios* went down to her by rope and stayed with her until the men were able to get them out.'

'Where is he now?' Chloe demanded, almost sagging with relief as she heard Leon's voice in the hallway.

She rushed to the top of the stairs, pausing transfixed as she looked down into the hallway below. Leon was standing there, holding Marisa in his arms in much the same fashion as he had her a handful of hours earlier, but now his face was grey and lined with exhaustion, the skin clinging to his bones in stark relief, the beginnings of a beard on his chin. He looked up and saw her and for one second Chloe could have sworn she saw tenderness and love in his eyes—however, if she had it was banished as the figure in his arms moved slightly, and Marisa lifted her head.

Her skin was the colour of Chloe's pearls, her eyes dark and bitter, her damp hair clinging to her face and throat.

'Chloe. . . .' Leon began, but before he could continue, Marisa whimpered sharply, 'No. . . . No, Leon, don't leave me—please, don't leave me!' her whole body trembling as she clung fiercely to his shoulders.

Her skirt and blouse were filthy and torn, and Chloe could see bruises forming on the too pale skin.

'It's all right, little one, I'm not going anywhere,' Leon soothed. 'Chloe, pack a change of clothes for both of you as quickly as you can. Marisa is in shock, and I want to get her to Athens as quickly as possible. We don't have any medical facilities on the island to cope with something like this. The helicopter is waiting. How long will you be?'

'Five minutes,' Chloe promised him, refusing to think about the hatred she had seen in Marisa's eyes when she had turned and seen her.

Her questions must wait until later; until Leon was rested and Marisa was in capable medical hands.

Chloe was as good as her word and within five minutes was back in the hall dressed in serviceable jeans and a warm sweat-shirt, a case at her side.

Spiro was waiting for her in the hall. Leon and

Marisa were already in the helicopter, he told her, and when Chloe got there she found Leon at the controls while Marisa, apparently asleep, was lying prone on two seats in the back.

'Keep an eye on her, will you?' Leon instructed Chloe. 'I've given her a tranquillising shot. Dr Livanos, whom I telephoned, told me it would be perfectly safe. It should last until we are able to get her to the hospital.'

'What happened?' Chloe asked him ten minutes later when they were airborne. The storm had abated with the coming of dawn and although rags of cloud still discoloured the sky, the sea below them was definitely calmer. 'Spiro said something about you finding Marisa in a cave. . . .'

'That's right.'

He vouchsafed no further information, concentrating on the helicopter's controls, his lips drawn together in a line which discouraged further conversation.

'But how ... how did she get there?' Chloe pursued, ignoring the warning signs. 'I thought she was walking along the cliffs—surely she didn't actually climb down them?'

'I don't know what she did,' Leon said crisply. 'Once I had found her all that concerned me was getting her to safety. The mouth of the cave had been sealed off by the sea, but luckily Marisa had found a ledge and crawled on to it. We wouldn't have found her if Spiro hadn't spotted her jacket hanging from a gorse bush halfway down the cliff face. We should be in Athens within the hour,' he added. 'I'll drive you straight to the apartment and then go on to the hospital with Marisa.'

Something was niggling at Chloe, something that was eluding her, and remaining annoyingly just out of reach, but in the face of Leon's obvious disinclination to discuss the matter further, she could hardly press him with more questions.

They continued the journey in silence. One of Leon's employees was waiting at the airport with a car to which they were ushered with the speed and lack of fuss that only great wealth and privilege achieve.

True to his promise, Leon took Chloe first to the apartment, where she had spent the brief months of her marriage.

Seeing it again brought back memories which she would far rather not have have resurrected, and she wandered from room to room as she waited for him to return, trying not to remember the ill-fated day on which Marisa had told her of her true relationship with him.

Marisa! That was it! That was what had been bothering her! It was as though Leon had not wanted to talk to her about finding Marisa, as though there was something he wanted to conceal from her!

Nonsense, she told herself firmly, she was letting her imagination run away with her.

It was late afternoon before Leon returned from the hospital. Dr Livanos wanted to keep Marisa in overnight, he told her, just to check up on her.

'I still don't understand what possessed her to go out for a walk in the first place,' Chloe commented in puzzlement. They were sitting in the drawing room, Leon lying back against the pale green upholstery, his eyes closed in weariness, a glass of whisky in one hand. 'It isn't exactly one of her favourite pastimes, in fact I thought she loathed walking.'

'Does it matter why?'

His eye flew open, the question terse, almost antagonistic and Chloe fought against a growing sense of unease.

'Not really,' she said lightly. She mustn't forget the strain he must have been under. 'I was just speculating really. Leon. . . .' instinct warned her that this was not the time for discussing the future, but all at once she had to know the truth. 'Leon, I know you want us to stay together, to provide a stable background for the children we could have, but there's something I have to ask you, something I have to know!'

Silence!

Chloe raised her head and looked across the room. Leon was still lying back against the cushions, his eyes closed, no sign of any reaction in his expression.

Desperately she plunged on. 'I know this isn't the best time to bring this up, but I have to ask you. What do you intend to do about Marisa?'

Still that unnerving silence.

She forced herself to look across at him, and as she lifted her head she heard a soft thud, and looked up just in time to see his glass slipping from his fingers and falling to the floor.

'*Leon!*'

She was on her feet and at his side, bewilderment giving way to mild hysteria as the truth dawned. Leon had fallen fast asleep! As she looked at him tenderness overwhelmed her and it no longer mattered that he hadn't heard or answered her question; that she didn't know what the future held;

nothing mattered but the overwhelming urge of love she felt for this man.

She made him as comfortable as she could, and instructed the staff not to disturb him, simply placing a duvet from the bedroom over his recumbent body, and gently closing the door behind her as she stepped out into the hall.

The phone ran several times during the evening— one of the calls was from the island, and Chloe assured Spiro that everything was under control. Several business acquaintances of Leon's called enquiring about Marisa's health. It was amazing how news travelled! And then about nine o'clock Madam Kriticos rang, but her concern was for Leon rather than his half-sister.

'You have still not taken my advice, I see,' she said to Chloe. 'Get rid of her, my dear, otherwise you will find you're nurturing a serpent in your bosom.'

If only she could, Chloe reflected as she replaced the receiver, smiling wryly as she contemplated the desirability of a fairy godmother who could wave her wand and set matters right.

At ten o'clock she returned to the drawing room to check on Leon. She was just bending over him, securing the duvet, when something alerted her to the fact that he was no longer asleep.

'Very nice,' he murmured drowsily with his lips against the base of her throat, 'but what the hell am I doing sleeping here?'

'You tell me,' Chloe responded dryly. 'Personally I put it down to exhaustion.'

'Mmm, I thought you'd grown brave all of a sudden. Trying to take advantage of a defenceless man!'

'I was not!' Chloe retorted indignantly. 'I was

trying to make you comfortable. You were so tired. . . .'

'Too tired to get up and walk into the bedroom,' Leon admitted ruefully, his eyes darkening suddenly as he added softly, 'Too tired to even undress myself. Will you do it for me?'

Chloe tried to control her reaction and failed, trembling betrayingly as Leon's mouth slid moistly along her throat, his hands locking behind her back as he pulled her gently down on top of him.

'Well?' he drawled huskily between kisses. 'Are you going to take pity on me and help me like a dutiful wife?'

'I suppose I'll have to.' She deliberately kept her voice neutral, her lashes concealing her expression from him, but nothing could hide the eagerness in her fingers as they curled against the warm vee of flesh exposed by his open-necked shirt. She tried to imitate his own cool control, deliberately hesitating before unfastening the first button, but all pretence was forgotten as Leon reached for her urgently, his voice thickening with desire as he muttered un- steadily, 'Oh, Chloe, I want you,' into the smooth creaminess of her throat.

After that there was no holding back. Chloe forgot where they were, what had happened, everything but the inciting warmth of Leon's body, of his proxi- mity, of his skin beneath her fingers and the urgent heat of his mouth as it claimed her own.

She had made one soft protest initially, but Leon had laughed aside her suggestion that someone might intrude upon them, and because she had had as little desire as Leon to withdraw from their embrace she had let her objections die.

'Oh, Chloe!'

She could feel the urgent pressure of his thigh muscles, the ragged uneven rasping of his breath, her body clamouring as passionately for fulfilment as did his. She was lost, drowning in a warm, bottomless well of pleasure, soaring mindlessly towards the clouds, her body already anticipating the exquisite moments of fulfilment.

'. . . Leon!' The interruption broke in upon their privacy.

Above her Chloe was aware of Leon moving, of him cursing, and hurriedly covering her with the duvet which had been lying disregarded on the floor, and she sat up unsteadily, her eyes widening in disbelief as she saw Marisa standing framed in the door, her face white with pain as she surveyed the all too betraying evidence of what she had interrupted.

'Leon, how could you?' she demanded bitterly. 'How could you be like this with her when I needed you?'

'For God's sake, Marisa. . . .' Chloe heard Leon begin tetchily, the tone of his voice sharpening to concern as Marisa turned, and fled. 'Marisa, wait!'

Chloe sat like a frozen marble statue as Leon pulled on his shirt and pants. She heard a bedroom door slam and guessed that it was Marisa's, although what the girl was doing out of hospital she could not imagine. She longed for Leon to speak to her, to offer her some words of tenderness and comfort; ridiculously, she felt like the 'other woman' caught out in some sordid, furtive lovemaking with someone else's husband, the shock of Marisa's sudden interruption making her shake with an inward tension that could only have found relief in the protection of Leon's arms. But that protection was not offered to her. Instead Leon pulled on his shoes and hurried after Marisa. To do what? Chloe wondered bitterly. To assure her that what she had inadvertently witnessed meant nothing?

She was already in bed when Leon came into their room an hour later.

'Is Marisa all right now?' she asked politely, forcing herself to sound calm and unconcerned.

'As far as I can tell. She discharged herself from hospital. She was on the verge of hysterics, so rather than force her to go back I telephoned Dr Livanos and got his sanction for her to stay here. Lord, I'm tired!' He massaged the back of his neck with lean fingers, flexing his shoulders wearily.

'Leon,' Chloe began impulsively, 'there's something we have to talk about . . . Marisa. . . .'

'For Pete's sake, not now. Tomorrow—we'll talk about it tomorrow. Right now all I want to do is sleep.'

And that was exactly what he did, while Chloe lay wide awake and tense at his side, wishing she knew what to believe. When she was in Leon's arms, everything else paled into insignificance, but she couldn't spend the rest of her life simply ignoring her own insecurity and fear.

It was a long time before she slept.

When she woke up it was several seconds before she realised that she was alone. She groped blindly along the other side of the bed to check that she was right, and then as her eyes accustomed themselves to the darkness she saw that Leon had thrown back the covers on his side when he had left her. She glanced at her watch. It was three o'clock in the morning. Some nameless dread made her clamber out of bed and walk towards the door, pushing it open like a sleepwalker.

Without actively thinking what she was doing Chloe walked slowly down the corridor. A thin strip of light showed under Marisa's bedroom door, and Chloe could hear the muted sound of voices from within. Like someone in the grip of a nightmare she turned the handle and opened the door.

Marisa was clasped in Leon's arms, the voluptuous curves of her body plainly visible in the soft light of the bedside lamp. Leon was sitting on her bed, his back to the door, his skin gilded to bronze by the lamp.

A terrible sickness seized Chloe by the throat, faintness overwhelming her as she clutched the door for support.

'Promise me you'll always love me, Leon,' she heard Marisa beg passionately. 'Promise me you'll send her away. I can't bear it if you don't. I want it to be like it used to be, just the two of us. . . .'

Leon's reply was lost as Marisa pressed her body wantonly against him, the full red lips against his cheek. Chloe didn't wait to hear any more. Somehow she managed to make her way back to her bedroom, the nausea which overwhelmed her in the bathroom leaving her drained and shaken.

What a fool she had been! What a stupid, romantic fool! Marisa had already told her why Leon wanted her back—because he wanted a son—but she had refused to believe it, had woven romantic illusions around herself, and if she was trapped within them now she had no one but herself to blame. Although she waited dry-eyed with an aching heart, Leon did not return, and when dawn crept palely over the sky, Chloe acknowledged at last that she had lost. No matter what degree of desire he might feel for her, Leon was not prepared to give up Marisa. The only question to remain was, did she have the stamina to endure that knowledge, year after year, watching her children grow up in the shadow of that tainted relationship, waiting for Marisa to try to destroy them as she had destroyed that other, unborn child? She knew the answer.

Leon unwittingly made it easier for her. He was in the dining room drinking coffee when she walked in, his hair damp from a recent shower, a business suit giving him an urbane look of sophistication.

He replaced his coffee cup as Chloe sat down, studying her pale face briefly for a few seconds before saying casually:

'I have business which will take me out for most of the day. Will whatever it was you wanted to speak to me about last night wait until I return?'

Chloe suppressed hysterical laughter. She had almost forgotten that! And of course she had her answer. Leon was scanning the headlines of a newspaper lying on the table, as though her reply mattered little to him either way. That knowledge lent her courage.

'No, I'm afraid it won't,' she said with a coolness to match his own. 'I'm sorry, Leon, but I've decided I can't stay with you. Oh, I realise what I'll be giving up. . . . But I realise as well that I can't compromise. Without love—real love, not merely passion or desire—I just can't see it working, and neither do I feel that it would be fair to subject children to the sort of relationship we would have.'

For a moment Leon was silent. While she spoke he had been folding his newspaper, sharpening the creases with his thumb, now he put it aside and looked directly at her.

'If that's the way you feel. . . .'

'It is. And I won't change my mind—under any circumstances!'

'Very well. I can see no point in prolonging matters. I'll check on the time of the first available flight to London, and book you a seat on it. Getting a divorce will of course be complicated by the fact that to all intents and purposes we have been "reconciled" for these last few weeks, and there's bound to be some element of delay. However, as soon as it can be arranged I promise you that I shall set you free.'

Free! Chloe bit back a protest, tempted even now to fling herself into his arms, to break through the polite mask of his features and plead with him to take her and keep her and to hell with the consequences. But of course she didn't. The British reticence Leon had mocked so often in the past restrained her, and she didn't know whether to be glad or sorry when he rose from the table, indicating that the conversation was over, the decision irreversibly made!

She was in her bedroom, trying to pack only what was absolutely essential, when Marisa walked in. The other girl looked pale but triumphant, her eyes going immediately to the open suitcase.

'You're leaving! Not before time! Leon might have desired you, but it is me he loves; I who will always come first,' she announced shrilly, her voice rising on the last words. 'He spent last night with me, coming from your cold embraces to the warmth of

my bed. I can give him what you never can. I understand him. We share the same blood.' She laughed
wildly as Chloe paled, her lips curling with contempt.
'It offends you when I talk of our close relationship,
does it not? Leon does not find it offensive,' she said
softly. 'Ask him!'

Since Leon had already confirmed that he had
booked her a seat on the early afternoon flight to
Heathrow, there remained only one small task for
Chloe to accomplish, and this she did before finally
leaving her room. She took the pearls Leon had given
her and placed them in the drawer of the dressing
table, tears blurring her eyes as she remembered with
what joy she had worn them.

To her surprise Leon himself insisted on driving
her to the airport. To make sure she actually left? she
couldn't help asking herself cynically.

They drove to the airport in silence. Leon parked
the car outside the main entrance and leaned across
to open the passenger door. Chloe shrank back instinctively, puzzled by the look of intense bitterness
darkening his eyes as he saw the gesture.

'Goodbye, Chloe,' he said tersely as he handed her
her ticket and case. 'You will understand, I think, if I
do not make the conventional gesture of wishing you
well.' He bent suddenly, possessing her mouth in a
hard, punishing kiss, and then abruptly straightened,
turning on his heel and leaving her alone in the busy
airport lounge.

She managed to stay dry-eyed until the plane took
off. A stewardess, noting her averted profile and
catching sight of her reflection in the window, tact-
fully left her alone, and as there was no one occupying

the adjacent seats there was no one to witness the tears coursing painfully down her cheeks, as she wept for the impossibility of her dreams ever coming true, while her heart ached for the man she had left behind.

CHAPTER TEN

IT was late autumn and there was a distinct chill in the air. Chloe was just emerging from Harrods, where she had been on a fruitless errand for her employer who had wanted a particular brand of French silk tights.

There was a suspicion of frost in the air; early would-be Christmas shoppers milled by the doors. Chloe sighed and glanced at her watch. Louise would be wondering what had happened to her, she had been gone over an hour. As she turned Chloe collided with a woman wearing a full-length mink. They both started to apologise at the same time, Chloe's face registering astonishment as she recognised Madam Kriticos.

The recognition was mutual.

'Chloe!' the older woman exclaimed, catching hold of the sleeve of Chloe's tweed coat. 'My dear, what a surprise! Are you in a hurry? I was just on my way to Fortnum's to rest my feet and enjoy a cup of their tea and one of their delicious pastries. Please join me.'

'I can't. I'm working for a novelist at the moment, and I'm already late. . . .'

'Working? But surely. . . .'

'I enjoy it,' Chloe said quickly, not wanting to tell the other woman that since her return from Greece she had never touched the money Leon sent her every month. Her tiny bedsitter, her clothes, her food, were all paid for out of the salary she earned working for

Louise Simmonds. 'And Louise is marvellous to work for.'

'Very well then, if you can't join me now, you must dine with me later. We are staying at the Savoy and tonight my husband has a business dinner, so you will be doing me a great favour if you will come.'

She was wise enough not to comment on Chloe's pale complexion and haunted eyes, and knowing that she had no valid reason for not accepting the second invitation, Chloe reluctantly agreed.

'Good. Until eight o'clock this evening, then.'

The mêlée by the door which had thrown them together swallowed up Madame Kriticos, leaving Chloe to cross the road alone, and look despairingly for a taxi to take her to her employer's apartment in Belgravia.

By the time she had managed to hail an empty taxi, Chloe was feeling both cross and tired, and wishing she had been able to produce a concrete reason for refusing Madame Kriticos' invitation. She even toyed with the idea of telephoning the Savoy and leaving a message cancelling the arrangement, but stubborn pride refused to allow her to do something which might make her appear to be a coward.

Louise was frowning over some reviews of her latest book when Chloe walked into her study, her greying hair elegantly styled to complement the faintly austere lines of her face.

'Just listen to this!' she commanded derisively, flicking scarlet-tipped fingers against the page of a magazine, as she started to read. ' "Louise Simmonds has once again produced an extremely polished product—a thriller as sophisticated and subtle as its author." Polished! How dare he insult me like that! I sweated blood and guts over that book, and he knows it damn him.'

Glancing over her employer's shoulder to read the name at the bottom of the page, Chloe suppressed a faint smile. Maxwell Gordon and Louise were old friends and adversaries.

'He also said it was sophisticated and subtle,' she pointed out, 'and you know as well as I do that if he'd praised you to the heavens you would still have found something to niggle about.'

'The trouble with you, my girl,' Louise commented wryly, placing the magazine on her desk, 'is that in two short months you've got to know me far too well. Far better, in fact, than I know you. That wedding ring, for instance. . . . . You always wear it, and yet I've never once heard you mention a husband.'

'Because there is nothing *to* mention,' Chloe said brittlely.

'No?' Louise raised her eyebrows disbelievingly. 'Well, it's your life, Chloe. Now don't prim up on me,' she coaxed. 'You know what I'm like whenever I sense a mystery, and I sense one within you, Chloe, but I do respect your very natural desire to keep your private life, my dear,' she added gently. 'It's just that sometimes I look up and see you looking through that window, and I know you're miles away.'

'I'm sorry. I'm also sorry to have to tell you that I wasn't able to get your stockings.'

'Damn!' Louise swore pungently. 'I'm dining with Geoffrey Lewis tonight—I pointed him out to you at that P.R. do last week. He could be interested in buying the rights of *Lie or Die* for a film. I could do with the money right now,' she added frankly, and Chloe, knowing that her employer had twin teenage sons currently attending an expensive public school, guessed that this was the reason why. Louise was a widow, but far from helpless, having carved out a career for herself in one of the toughest businesses in the world, and there was nothing she would not do for her two sons.

'I badly wanted to look my best,' Louise added.

'Wear Dior ones,' Chloe suggested, adding wickedly, 'He won't be able to tell the difference just by looking! I suppose you want me to stay on and finish what you've done while I've been out,' she added carelessly, thinking it would be a perfect excuse for not meeting Madame Kriticos, but Louise shook her head firmly.

'You've already worked late twice this week, and that's more than enough. And you're losing weight, and yet. . . .' She frowned thoughtfully. 'We've only worked together for two months, Chloe, but in that time I've become very fond of you. If you have any problems, or just need a sympathetic ear, I hope you can always come to me.'

'The tough novelist who's really as soft as butter,' Chloe teased, but she was touched by Louise's offer. However, the past was over, and the surest way to make sure it stayed behind her was to put it out of her mind and refuse to think about it.

She deliberately dawdled over tidying up her desk, reluctant to leave and commit herself to the first step towards the evening ahead. Louise had long since disappeared upstairs to prepare for her date, and at last when she knew she had no possible excuse for remaining any longer, Chloe pulled on her coat and hurried outside.

As luck would have it an empty taxi was cruising

past, and within minutes of leaving Belgravia she was
in her own bedsitter in a far less salubrious part of the
city.

The chill in the air had sharpened; she seemed to
be feeling the cold far more intensely since her return
from Greece, and for that reason she dressed in a
silky jersey dress in a matt black fabric, with long
sleeves. The rich cloth accentuated the silver-fairness
of her hair and the purple darkness of her eyes, but
she had lost weight, Chloe acknowledged, idly
smoothing an inch of slack fabric across her hips.

It was half past seven when she opened her wardrobe and pulled out a cream wool jacket. No mink
for her. She had had one, a beautiful coat which
Leon had bought for her in Paris, choosing the skins
himself, but she had left it behind her in Athens, the
first time.

Once again she had no problem with a taxi, and it
was just eight o'clock when she stepped into the foyer
of the Savoy and asked for Madame Kriticos.

'You came! I am so glad,' the older woman
beamed, when Chloe was shown to her table—set
discreetly in a semi-private alcove, and yet with an
excellent view of the rest of the restaurant. 'I thought
you might have had . . . what is it you call it? Ah yes,
I have it. Cold feet!'

'I did,' Chloe heard herself admitting wryly, 'but I
still came.'

'I am glad.' The Greek woman reached across the
table, covering Chloe's slender fingers with her own
plumper, bejewelled ones.

'You still wear your wedding ring,' she commented
quietly. 'We heard, of course, that you had left
Athens. No,' she said quickly as Chloe opened her

mouth to speak, 'no, do not say anything. I asked you to dine with me because I wanted your company, not because I wanted to pry insensitively into your private life. Now, shall we order? I must tell you that we now have high hopes of Nikos becoming betrothed to a charming girl—that is one of the reasons we are here in London—that and the shops. I love them, but oh, the cold!'

She talked about Athens, comparing the shops there with those in London; their main course arrived and Chloe, who had enjoyed her lemon sole, suddenly found her appetite vanishing as Madame Kriticos said chattily, 'Marisa is still unmarried. I doubt Leon will ever get rid of her now. She seems determined to disgrace him. Of course, the trouble is that she has been spoilt quite ridiculously. Are you not hungry?' she asked ingenuously, looking at Chloe's pale face. 'My dear, you don't look at all well, and you have lost weight,' she commented, inadvertently repeating Louise's observation. 'If you will forgive me for saying so,' she added forthrightly, 'neither you nor Leon looks any better for your separation—far from it. The last time I saw him he looked worn to death—all Marisa's fault, I am sure.'

Chloe pushed her food away almost untouched, turning her head and biting hard on her lips to prevent the betraying tears, which had formed the moment her companion mentioned Leon, from falling.

'Oh Chloe . . . my dear, I'm so sorry!' Madame Kriticos apologised, deftly angling her own chair so that none of the other diners could witness Chloe's distress, at the same time proffering a dainty lawn handkerchief edged with delicate lace. 'I never intended to be so tactless. I told myself that I wouldn't mention Leon. . . . You still love him, don't you?' she added softly.

Chloe wanted to deny it, but her tears, plus the fact that she simply could not form the words, betrayed her. All she could do was nod her head.

'It is all Marisa's fault,' Madame Kriticos announced energetically. 'I am sure of it, just as I am sure that Leon would welcome you back. . . .'

'No!' The word sounded louder than Chloe had intended, and she was aware of other diners glancing across at them. 'No . . . no, it just isn't possible,' she said in a lower voice. 'I can't talk about it . . . I. . . .'

To her horror she felt nausea overwhelming her, coupled with an enervating feeling of faintness.

'I don't feel very well,' she managed to whisper as Madame Kriticos' face swam hazily in front of her. 'I must have drunk too much wine.'

To her relief the sickness and dizziness started to fade almost immediately. Madame Kriticos wanted to summon the hotel doctor, but Chloe refused, privately believing that they had been caused by nerves and too much rich food. To her relief Madame Kriticos did not mention Leon again, but although the evening passed pleasantly enough Chloe found it hard to concentrate entirely on her companion, her thoughts returning again and again to Leon. It was always a mistake to start probing a still tender wound, she told herself later, preparing for bed, and especially a wound like hers, which seemed in danger of never healing.

It was a relief to learn from Louise the following day that the novelist had promised to visit some

friends living near York, and that she wanted Chloe
to go with her.

'It will be very much of a working weekend,' she
apologised. 'Richard is a lecturer at York University
and I've promised to give a talk on the merits of
modern literature. It promises to be a lively discussion
and I'd like you along to help me with some notes.
You're excellent at that sort of thing—far better than
me. It must be your advertising training. Do you
ever hanker after that life?' she asked casually. 'You
must find working for me quite a change.'

'It is a change,' Chloe agreed, 'but not one that I
regret.'

She was thinking in particular of Derek, who had
so neatly and callously led her into the trap Leon
had prepared.

The weekend went well. The Davidsons were a
pleasant easygoing couple in their mid-forties, who
lived in a rambling Victorian rectory several miles
outside York itself, together with an assortment of
children, dogs and ponies. Apart from the brief per-
iods when she was helping Louise with her notes,
Chloe was able to relax—or at least relax as much as
she could. Her appetite was still almost negligible,
and on the Sunday, while she was helping Mary
Davidson prepare the lunch, she was astounded when
the older woman said cheerfully:

'It seems unfair to let you help me prepare all this,
when you don't feel like eating anything. Wait until
a little later on, though, you'll find your appetite
comes back with a vengeance. I was just the same
with each of mine. . . .'

She was just in time to catch the pan of sprouts
Chloe had been preparing, and having neatly fielded

the vegetables unhurriedly pushed Chloe down into a comfortable chair and said practically:

'I take it you *are* pregnant? I recognised the symptoms straight away, especially when Louise commented that although you'd been losing weight, your face seemed to be fuller.'

Pregnant! Chloe did some rapid mental arithmetic and closed her eyes. How could she have been so blind, so unaware! That nausea the other night, her faintness, her general feeling of dragging tiredness, and the whole host of tiny but telling symptoms she ought to have recognised straight away.

'I didn't know,' she admitted, 'but I suspect you're right.'

'I'm sure I am. Like I said, having had five of my own, I know all the symptoms upside down and inside out. Louise tells me that you're separated from your husband?'

'Yes, we're going to get a divorce,' Chloe said briefly, aware of the older woman watching her.

'Umm, and the present situation could rather complicate things?'

'Not to the extent where I would want to change it,' Chloe said quietly.

Pregnant! Even now she could hardly believe it. They had been back in London a week and the first thing she had done had been to visit her own doctor. This morning she had received confirmation of her pregnancy. She had told Louise, who typically had said, 'Well, as far as I'm concerned it need not make any difference. You're the best secretary I've ever had— we get on well together too, so well in fact that I've been contemplating asking you if you'd care to move in here with me. You know how I am—working at odd hours and so forth. It could work out quite well, and needless to say, the offer includes Junior when he or she arrives.'

Chloe could have wept. Instead she grinned and said huskily, 'Wait until you've been kept awake for half a dozen nights on the run—you might feel differently then!'

'I'm willing to take that chance if you are, Chloe. I know myself well enough now to know I won't marry again. The twins are growing up, and I'm too gregarious to want to live alone. Are you going to let the father know?' Louise asked casually.

Was she? It was a question that tormented Chloe over the next few days. Leon had a right to know, she acknowledged, but she could not go back to him, not knowing what she did, and if she knew Leon he would move heaven and earth to try to secure custody of his child, and that was something she could not tolerate. She knew that she could, of course, reveal exactly why she had left him, but somehow she shrank from using such distasteful measures. She was still worrying at the problem the morning the letter arrived.

The envelope was thick, white and very expensive. Her name was typed on the front, and that of a firm of solicitors printed on the back. Chloe opened it, reaching unsteadily for a chair as she read it. Leon was going ahead with their divorce. She was to present herself at Suite 104 of the Ritz tomorrow when a representative of Leon's solicitors would discuss with her the procedure to be adopted to obtain the divorce.

If Louise found her rather preoccupied she made no comment, and it was only the tiredness which engulfed Chloe every evening now that allowed her to sleep. Even so she was awake early, dressing with far more care than the interview merited. She was ready much too early, unable to face anything more than a cup of tea, and decided to use the underground and then walk through the park, rather than take a taxi.

There had been frost during the night and leaves crunched underfoot as she walked across the grass. The park was empty, and she lingered for a few minutes, trying to prepare herself for the coming ordeal—and it would be an ordeal to hear from the lips of a stranger how her marriage was to be set aside, destroyed as though it had never been.

She was early, but rather than wait in the foyer she crossed to the reception desk and gave her name.

'Of course. You are expected. If you would just come this way. . . .'

Chloe was escorted to a lift which soared effortlessly upwards, stopping silently with a barely perceptible jerk.

Outside the door to the suite the porter smiled at her before knocking, then turned and left. By the time the door opened, the lift door was closing, and Chloe, her mouth dry with nervous tension, forced a formal smile to her lips as she stepped inside the suite.

She had a brief impression of cream carpet, and dark leather chesterfields, velvet curtains framing the huge expanse of plate glass windows, and then the room and everything in it faded from her mind, as the door closed behind her and Leon stepped away from it and took hold of her arm.

'You! What are you doing here?'

She was turning back as she spoke, reaching blindly

for the handle, but Leon was too quick for her, his body blocking her exit as he leaned negligently against the door, arms folded across his chest. He had obviously just showered and his hair was still damp, curling at the nape. His skin smelled of soap and beneath the fine silk shirt Chloe could see the dark shape of his body.

'How could you do this to me?' she demanded huskily, pride forgotten in the shock of seeing Leon in place of the solicitor she had expected. 'Haven't you done enough?'

'Not half as much as I'd like to,' Leon groaned, moving with the swiftness of a panther, almost jerking her off her feet as he hauled her into his arms. 'Tell me you don't want me,' he said softly, 'that you don't love me, and I'll walk out of this room and never contact you again.'

His lips were the merest hair's breadth from hers. Chloe swallowed painfully.

'I don't want you. I don't love you.' How it hurt to say the words!

'Liar!' His thumb caressed the line of her jaw, stroking the sensitive skin. 'You told Christina Kritikos that you did.'

Chloe's breath seemed to die in her throat.

'There's only one way to find out. Kisses can't lie, can they?' Leon murmured before his mouth covered hers. 'Which is something I ought to have realised before.'

Chloe tried to resist, to fight the drugging longing that swept through her at his touch, but her body betrayed her, her mouth opening between the sorcery of Leon's like the petals of a flower welcoming the sun. Her arms crept round his neck of her own volition, and she was unaware that she was crying until he touched her damp face with tender fingers.

'Now tell me you don't love me.'

'I can't,' Chloe admitted. 'Oh, Leon, why did you have to do this? Pride? Punishment? If you had any feelings for me, you would set me free....'

'You think so?' All at once he was breathing harshly. 'It's just because I do have "feelings" for you, as you put, that I can't. My, Chloe, do you have the remotest conception of what it meant to me to hear that you actually cared about me? *Loved* me, and hearing it too when all hope had gone, when I had forced myself to admit that I had lost you, that....' His fingers tightened painfully on her arms. He leaned forward resting his forehead against her, and she felt the dampness of his perspiration.

'Why do you think I've come half way across the world if I don't have "feelings" for you? "Feelings!" My word, you British! I love you, Chloe, you haunt my days and nights, tormenting me when you're there with your aloofness and tormenting me when you're not with your absence. Letting me believe that you never cared a damn about me!'

'You love *me*?' Try as she might, she couldn't quite keep the disbelief out of her voice. 'Leon! But Marisa....'

'No, don't say it,' he said quietly, his fingers on her lips. 'Come and sit down, Chloe, I want to talk to you. There's something I have to tell you.'

Obediently she followed him to one of the leather chesterfields, sitting primly at his side her hands folded neatly in childlike fashion. Leon sat down beside her, his face grave.

'Marisa died last night.'

Whatever else Chloe had been expecting it was not this, and she acted instinctively and generously, her arms opening wide to hold Leon to her, her eyes compassionate as she looked down at the dark head pillowed against her breast.

'Thank you for that,' Leon said unevenly, several seconds later. 'It was generous of you, Chloe, but then I never doubted your generosity. You know I told you that Marisa's mother died when she was a child?' he added. Chloe nodded, allowing him to take her in his arms, and treacherously enjoying the steady beat of his heart beneath her cheek. 'What I didn't tell you, and ought to have done, was that she took her own life. She had always been a little unstable, but after Marisa's birth she seemed to grow much worse. My father tried desperately to pretend she was merely highly strung, but it was more than that—much more,' he said heavily. 'She drowned herself when Marisa was barely two. When my father knew he was dying he made me promise that I would always look after Marisa. He was afraid for her, you see, afraid that she might have inherited her mother's instability.

'I thought she had escaped it. Oh, of course there were tantrums, scenes, but I put them down to adolescent growing pains. Even after our marriage, even when you told me that she had destroyed our child, I refused to recognise the truth—perhaps because I was not strong enough to face it, I don't know. I knew that Marisa was jealous of you, and God forgive me, I thought perhaps that you were jealous of her. You were so young, you see, and I knew I had rushed you into marriage before you were ready for it—because I was terrified that if I did not I might lose you to someone else. I fell in love with you the moment I saw you, but you were so young . . . so very young, I daren't let you see how I felt about you in case the intensity of my emotions frightened you off. I hoped that love for me would grow slowly.

Chloe checked a small protest, surprised that Leon, who had always seemed so invincible, had had doubts, just as she had herself; had not known that almost from the first moment she had seen him she had fallen deeply in love with him—as he apparently had done with her! Leon was still talking, his voice low and filled with pain.

'When you left me,' he went on, 'I cursed myself for driving you away. I wanted to come after you, but pride held me back, and then by the time my longing for you overcame my pride, matters had gone too far, so I decided to devise some other means of getting you back. I told myself that I had every right to demand from you the son you had stolen from me, but underneath . . . underneath it was you I wanted, Chloe. When Marisa told me you had only married me for my wealth I think I lost my mind for a short time. She deceived us both too easily, perhaps because neither of us had let the other see deep into our hearts.

'I suppose I should have guessed what she was doing. She was strangely exalted after you left me the first time, but in the interim period she grew much calmer—so much calmer that I decided I could take the risk of looking for a suitable husband for her—someone like Nikos, kind and gentle. I didn't realise then that a husband was the last thing she wanted! She was so hysterical on Eos that I began to get seriously worried about her—that was why I was so

determined to return to the island when I learned
that she was missing. I was forcing myself to admit
that she was not as stable as I had pretended, but
even then I never dreamed that she had actually told
you that she and I were lovers. Before you and I left
Eos I told her that I hoped to persuade you to agree
that you and I could try again, and I thought she
was just being hysterical, when she demanded that I
didn't. Even so, when I heard she was missing my
first thought wasn't that she might have done
something foolish—until I saw her jacket. I knew
then that the whole thing was a deliberate ploy to
distract my attention from you to her, but even then
I didn't realise *why*. And then you changed your mind
and said you were leaving me. I felt I must let you
go, that I couldn't hold on to you against your will.

'When Christina Kriticos told me that she had
seen you in London and that you had told her that
you still loved me, I hardly dared believe it. I told
Marisa that I intended coming over here to bring
you back with me. She had hysterics, and told me
that she'd kill herself if I brought you back. I had to
call in Dr Livanos. He told me that he thought she
was seriously disturbed, and for her own sake I agreed
that she should go into hospital for some tests. Since
the night she discharged herself from hospital her
behaviour had grown very odd. I was called out of
Athens on business, and apparently during my absence she simply walked out of hospital. She was
knocked down and seriously injured by a speeding
car as she left the hospital grounds. By the time I got
to her bedside they knew there was no hope for her.
She was barely conscious when I arrived. I think she
realised it too, because she told me the truth. How

she had misled you into believing that there was an incestuous relationship between us; that I had deliberately seduced her— None of it was ever true, Chloe. I loved her, yes, but as a sister, nothing more! She told me how she had managed to persuade you to believe that I had married you to provide a smoke-screen for my affair with her—that was when I realised how clever she had been, how utterly convincing, and I cursed myself for putting pride before truth and not telling you all along how much you meant to me. She told me about your fall, about how jealous she had been because you were carrying my child—I could hardly believe I was hearing the truth. She claimed she did it out of love for me—Love! It was a sickness—an obsession.'

'She told me that the only reason you wanted me back was because you wanted a child,' said Chloe, speaking for the first time, 'and it seemed to tie in so neatly with what you had said. . . . I wanted to demand that you tell me if you were going to give her up—but I lacked the courage!'

'Of course I wanted a child—our child,' Leon said roughly, 'but not anything like as much as I want you—never think that. The child was just an excuse—I thought if you did conceive it would be another means of keeping you with me.' He cupped her face with his hands, the light falling full on his features so that Chloe could see the disillusionment and exhaustion there. You'll never know what it cost me to take you to the airport—to let you leave without begging you to stay. You do believe me, don't you, Chloe?'

She nodded her head slowly. 'And I don't think Marisa would have taken her own life. Try to believe that, Leon.'

'I think you're right, but even now I can hardly reconcile the sister I though I knew with the woman she actually was—a woman who would stop at nothing, obsessed almost to the point of fanaticism. . . .'

'If she was disturbed in some way, it could be that she was two separate women,' Chloe said softly. 'You must remember her as the sister you loved, Leon, and nothing else.'

'And you will come back to Greece and live with me?'

She gave him a shaky smile. 'Try and stop me! I've missed you so much,' she said simply. 'So, very, very much.'

'Not half as much as I've missed you.' He lifted her up in his arms and walked across the sitting room, kicking open the door to what was obviously his bedroom. 'I want you, Chloe,' he said unsteadily. She met his eyes without pretence or restraint and murmured against the warmth of his mouth, 'And I want you. . . .'

She knew as instinctively as she knew that he was telling her the truth about Marisa that his need of her now was probably greater than it had ever been at any previous time. There would be few occasions during their life together when he would need her to be the stronger, to be able to turn to her for succour and tenderness, but Chloe knew that this was one of them, and she gave herself unstintingly to him. Later there would be time to tell him about the child she carried, for now he needed her all to himself, and she made a silent vow to herself that she would not let Marisa's deceit cast a shadow over his life.

'Love me, Chloe,' he groaned, his mouth against her breast, the heavy warmth of his thighs creating a pleasant lethargy within her. 'Love me and let me love you, without any barriers or fears between us.'

In answer Chloe reached up towards him, her heart in her eyes, the fierce pressure of his mouth making any other means of communication completely unnecessary. They had known unhappiness and pain; now it was their time to know love.

Harlequin® Plus

A WORD ABOUT THE AUTHOR

Penny Jordan loved the scene in the movie *Kramer vs Kramer* in which the hero mentions "one of the best five days" of his life because she well remembers one of her own best five. It was the day Mills & Boon accepted her first novel.

As a child in Preston, a small city north of Liverpool, England, where she was born, she was constantly in trouble for daydreaming, a trait she shares with a good number of her fellow authors. She also spent countless hours curled up with books and, when she was a teenager, began to read romances avidly.

But it wasn't until she was thirty and wanted to do something uniquely her own that she decided to try her hand at writing. At first, even her best ideas ended up in the wastebasket because she had not yet learned to carry an idea through from start to finish. Time and hard work paid off, though, and resulted in that first acceptance letter—and others that were to follow.

Now Penny works full-time on her writing—she was until recently a secretary—and she feels deeply grateful to be able to do something that gives such pleasure, not only to her, but to millions of romance readers.

Take these
4 best-selling novels
FREE

Yes! Four sophisticated, contemporary love stories by four world-famous authors of romance FREE, as your introduction to the Harlequin Presents subscription plan. Thrill to **Anne Mather**'s passionate story BORN OUT OF LOVE, set in the Caribbean.... Travel to darkest Africa in **Violet Winspear**'s TIME OF THE TEMPTRESS....Let **Charlotte Lamb** take you to the fascinating world of London's Fleet Street in MAN'S WORLD ....Discover beautiful Greece in **Sally Wentworth**'s moving romance SAY HELLO TO YESTERDAY.

Harlequin Presents...

The very finest in romance fiction

Join the millions of avid Harlequin readers all over the world who delight in the magic of a really exciting novel. EIGHT great NEW titles published EACH MONTH! Each month you will get to know exciting, interesting, true-to-life people .... You'll be swept to distant lands you've dreamed of visiting .... Intrigue, adventure, romance, and the destiny of many lives will thrill you through each Harlequin Presents novel.

Get all the latest books before they're sold out!
As a Harlequin subscriber you actually receive your personal copies of the latest Presents novels immediately after they come off the press, so you're sure of getting all 8 each month.

Cancel your subscription whenever you wish!
You don't have to buy any minimum number of books. Whenever you decide to stop your subscription just let us know and we'll cancel all further shipments.